Rockhaven
Christmas

Farley Dunn

THREE SKILLET

ROCKHAVEN CHRISTMAS, Dunn, Farley L

First Edition

A Katie Carver Novel

THREE SKILLET

www.ThreeSkilletPublishing.com

v.2

All characters are fictitious, and any resemblance to actual persons living or dead is purely coincidental.

ISBN 978-1-943189-05-2

Enjoy all the Katie Carver novels:

Rockhaven Summer

Rockhaven Wedding

Rockhaven Christmas

Rockhaven Spring

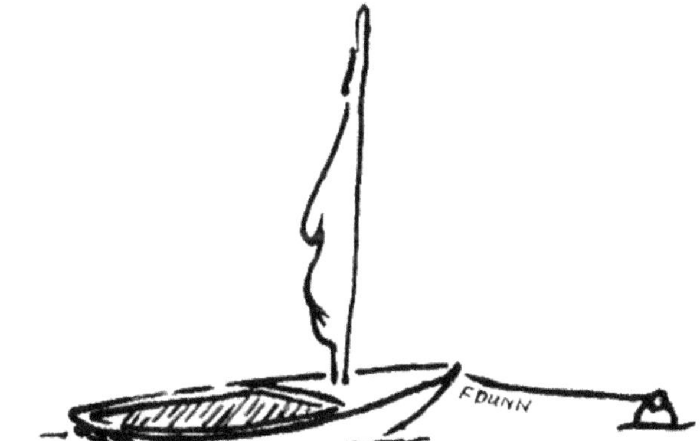

Author's Note

Those of you familiar with Mid-Coast Maine will recognize elements of Vinalhaven Island in my Rockhaven series, but only because of my family history and the summers I've spent there. If you do visit Vinalhaven someday, look for Rockhaven. You'll find that magical place strewn all about the craggy shoreline and in the stalwart people that call Vinalhaven home.

1

The languid aroma of wood smoke filled Katie Carver Ragsdale's dreams, and she smiled as she imagined a plump, lightly browned turkey roasting over an open fire. At the sizzle and pop of dripping fat, her stomach rumbled, and in her dreams, apple and cherry and pumpkin pies floated around the room.

Her guests raised their glasses in a toast, downing their eggnog in a single draught before tossing Katie's new stemware into the stone fireplace and shattering glass all over her perfectly roasted turkey.

Katie's eyes jerked open, and she felt the chill in the room as she waited for her breath to slow. It was dark, still, meaning the sun wasn't up. The snowstorm yesterday had become a blizzard, and before the phone lines had gone down, they'd learned the town storage facility had lost half its roof. Jeff had shaken his head, remarking that if the wind was pulling off roofs, he hoped everyone's boats survived.

He'd also reassured Katie that their property being on the east side of the island provided a great deal of protection. His family's old home place being on Moffat Cove gave them one of the best moorings around, second only to the ones in Rockhaven Harbor.

Katie tossed the bedding aside, and she searched with her feet for her slippers. The floor would be cold without them. With the electricity off, too, there wouldn't be any heat until she got a fire built in the fireplace.

Even their backup generator had failed to kick on, leaving them totally in the dark.

When she only found cold wood, she grumbled, "Generators need backup, too," remembering commercials for emergency units that worked seamlessly in all the television ads. And with the storm, Jeff couldn't go retrieve the one out on Carver Point. Three feet of snow told all there was to say about that.

She looked to the other side of the bed to where Jeff was lying, bundled for warmth. The bed could be empty for all she knew, it was so dark. Even her phone was dead, used up for lighting while Jeff struggled last night to get the generator online.

She sniffed, drawing in a long breath. She hadn't dreamed it. It was really there. Wood smoke. And turkey. In that she remembered what day it was. Thanksgiving, and all the plans that had been canceled, shattered by the unexpected change in the weather.

Standing and pulling her sensible—and very

warm—flannel nightgown tighter at the neck, she became aware of a shimmer of light orange flickering underneath the bedroom door. Her heart thumped at that. Had the fire been dampened properly the night before? Surely the house was not on fire.

"Jeff," she whispered hoarsely, afraid that to say it was to make it true. When he didn't answer, she called again, louder. "Jeffrey."

That would get his attention. She never called him Jeffrey. He hated it for reminding him of being a boy, and how badly he'd wanted to grow and become a man. He laughed when he said that, but he also made sure everyone knew he was serious.

"Jeff, there's a fire in the other room. I think the house might be on fire." She worked to his side of the bed and felt for him beneath the covers. It was lumpy, and she poked farther and farther up the bed. Something beyond the door popped loudly, like green wood in a campfire, and she gasped in alarm.

"Jeff, where are you?" Her eyes had begun to burn with impending tears. He had to be here.

A knock on the bedroom door caused her to jump.

"Katie? You up?" Then the door was silent.

"Jeff?" She called louder, making one last broad sweep of the bed with her outstretched hand. "Is that you?"

"No, it's Roker, here on snowshoes. Of course, it's me. Who else would it be? Come in here where it's warm." There was laughter behind the invitation.

"Coming." She pulled her hair from her face, pushing it behind her ears. So. That was why she hadn't been able to find him in the bedding. He wasn't in the bedding. Opening the door, she was hit by a wave of smoky, turkey-laced warmth. A fire indeed crackled in the big stone fireplace. Jeff was at the front door, pulling thick gloves off. He was bundled in jeans—double layered by the look of them—with a thick turtleneck sweater in a pale merino wool. His hair was a giant, flyaway mane of outdoors abandon, and just the barest hint of a beard shadowed his jawline. Big boots on his feet completed the Maine outdoorsman effect.

"You've been busy this morning." One tell-tale sign was the damp ring at the bottom of his jeans. He had been outdoors, already, and probably more than once. With the fresh pile of wood, some still showing snow, outside maybe five or six times.

"Good morning, Katie." He smiled at her, and deep crevasses dimpled the slabs of his cheeks. "Be sure to pull the door to. No need to heat the bedroom."

"Oh, right. I didn't think." She turned to close it. When she clicked it shut, she backed up, only to find Jeff right there.

"Good morning, again, Katie." He wrapped his arms around her, and he buried his face in her hair, to nuzzle her along her neck. "I like telling you good morning. And don't worry about the door. Who can think after a night spent in a storm like this? You're becoming a true Mainer."

"Yeah," and she laughed, pushing him away to make it towards the warmth of the fire. "I leap in bed and sleep through it all. A true Mainer, right. I smell turkey, and it's not my imagination. It reminds me I need real food. Breakfast-type food. With no electricity, I suppose we're skipping that today."

"Turkey's the best. It's Thanksgiving. What can I say? Can't have Thanksgiving without turkey. And you don't have to skip breakfast." He looked amused as he took the poker and brushed aside some of the coals at the back of the fire. Buried inside was a large covered Dutch oven. He pulled out a smaller Dutch oven and brushed the coals off the top. He piled them back around the bigger one.

"The whole turkey?" It had been the biggest they could buy. Half the church membership had planned to share it. "We'll never eat all that."

"Someone will." He didn't seem concerned, still working with the smaller oven, and with the poker, lifting the lid. Off to the side was a stack of several paper napkins.

"How long do you need to leave it in there? And that smells good. What's in that?"

"I don't know how long to leave the turkey, but this is about ready. What do you think?" He dipped with a large spoon and worked out a steaming cinnamon roll. "Want to share?"

He wrapped the bottom half in one of the napkins and brought it to her. Wrapping his arms around her again, he tore off a portion and held it to her mouth, waiting as she pulled it from his fingers. His next words were soft in her ear. "Maybe we should leave the turkey all day, and we can snuggle on the sofa while it cooks. By tonight, it'll fall off the bone. Pulled turkey, how does that sound?"

"Like I'm freezing. I need to get dressed. Oh, and do we have any water?" Snuggling! The roll was good, but she was suddenly aware she had other needs. Morning ones. And no matter the fire, it was still cold. Jeff might be bundled up, but she was wearing her nightgown. Even flannel wasn't enough to ward off the chill of the worst winter storm she remembered in years, especially in a house with no power. Added to that, she hadn't found her slippers, and her toes were starting to hurt.

Jeff looked at her and shook his head, as if she should know the answer to that.

"No?"

"I drew up what I could before it froze. We can use what's in the tub to flush, as long as it doesn't freeze, and there's drinking water in the kitchen. Don't plan on a shower unless I can get the generator running. Welcome to Maine, Dame Carver."

"Dame Ragsdale." It had been less than two months, and Ragsdale still fit awkwardly against her first name, but she wasn't letting go of it. She might be Dame Carver to Jeff, but she wanted it very clear. Dame Ragsdale was here to stay.

"Ah, that's right. We did have a wedding, didn't we?" He chuckled softly. "Your clothes are on the stool by the fire. I thought you might enjoy wearing them preheated."

"Oh, I am so lucky to have you." Katie turned and embraced him, and with her hands on his face, she kissed him passionately.

"Maybe it's too early for you to get dressed." He

smiled, but he chuckled suggestively, too, just enough that it was there.

"You fool. I'm freezing. I'm getting dressed, and now. Have some of that turkey waiting on me when I get back. I'm starving." She darted away, grabbed the clothes, and headed to the bathroom. When she closed the door, she was pleasantly surprised to see two pillar candles burning merrily away.

Jeff had thought of everything. He was so wonderful. Now if he could get that generator fixed, maybe they could have a proper Thanksgiving. It had to happen today, too, because tomorrow? Tomorrow was the first day of her upcoming Christmas schedule.

As Katie pulled on her long johns, she saw the card she'd slipped into the edge of the mirror the night before. It had been in her jeans pocket, and in the dark she'd been afraid she'd lose it. It had the upcoming month marked out by the day.

Looking at the card, she felt December coming apart in her head. It was Christmas in four weeks, and she had the biggest holiday of the year to plan. With a blizzard shutting down the entire island, her card filled with plans was now worthless for anything except a drink coaster.

Taking a deep breath, she laced her shoes and pulled on her double-lined sweatshirt. She might not look beautiful today, but she would be warm. Pulling the card from the mirror, she slipped it into her back pocket, determined not to let a month full of unraveling plans ruin her morning. It was Thanksgiving, her first one on the island ever, and she was spending it with Jeff. How wonderful was that?

When she stepped back into the warmth, Jeff was at the fire adding wood, and in the flickering shadows of the room, silhouetted against the flames, he was picture perfect.

"Perfect Christmas scene." Katie held her hands out, framing him in a box built of her fingers. "You should be on all our Christmas cards."

"Perfect Thanksgiving scene. Don't rush today away. Remember, we get to spend it together." He stood, and he walked to her. "You are so beautiful. I am the luckiest man in the world."

"Oh, you—" she started.

"Don't you 'oh, you' me. I waited on you half my life, and God brought you back to Rockhaven. He's done more for me than I ever deserved."

What could Katie say to that except agree? It was the way she felt every single day. Instead of answering, she pulled him to her and gave him a second Thanksgiving kiss, this one longer and more enjoyable than before.

It was the least she could do for the man who had completed her life, including building a fire and roasting her Thanksgiving turkey.

It would be her best Thanksgiving ever, bar none, and not even worrying over her plans for Christmas would get in the way.

2

"Jeff, I think that was a knock at the door." Katie rubbed the drowsiness from her eyes. She was snuggled next to him under a thick blanket, and the fire across the room crackled merrily. Jeff had piled it high with wood, and they'd moved the sofa close to maximize the warmth.

Now? She was very toasty, and she didn't want anything to disturb her cocoon of comfort.

"Nah," he replied, yawning. He shifted next to her, and his arm around her waist pulled her tighter. "The house is creaking. It does that in cold weather."

Katie moved the blanket enough that she could peer outside. Expansive windows wrapped the three walls facing the water. This might very well be a fisherman's abode, but someone in the past had remodeled it to take in the view of Moffat Cove. Once the dawn had peeked in around the blinds, Jeff had pulled them all up to allow as much light in as possible. With the omnipresent cloud cover, it was limited, but with all the glass, it was sufficient.

It was snowing again, and from time to time, Katie could see the smoke from the fireplace drift by in stained, cotton-candy puffs, all strung together like a giant caterpillar with uneven sections. The ground was white down to the sea, and the dock and Jeff's boat were draped in wedding-cake bliss. Even the ocean seemed thick and creamy, as it churned against the remains of last night's storm.

The knock repeated itself.

"Jeff, there really is someone at the door." It was an impossible knock in this isolated world of snow and quiet. The only sounds came from the fire, and that knock, of course.

"Okay. I'll check." He threw back the blanket and disentangled himself from Katie. "Maybe it's a pumpkin pie."

"I wish." That was one thing Katie hadn't prepared for. She had promises from multiple cooks, all much better at pies than she. Now? She didn't guess many pies were making it across the island today.

"We'll see." He kissed her on the forehead and stood, making his way to the front door, a massive slab filled with the original beveled glass from when the house was built, and into the enclosed and unheated foyer. Good for this time of year, he'd said proudly when she'd asked why it was kept closed off. It was also where they stored their outdoor clothing to keep it out of the house as it dried.

Katie heard voices, and she shook her head, sitting up and running her fingers through her hair. She glanced that way to see another man with Jeff. Who? He was so bundled up that in the dim light she couldn't tell. It could be almost anyone. Maine islanders were tough people who would get out in anything. In Boston? They'd wait for the plows, and if, if they could get to their cars, they'd be out again. For a fact no plows had come down Jeff and Katie's drive, not on Thanksgiving, and certainly not at this fresh hour of the morning.

The door opened, and Jeff came in laughing, followed by Roker, a good friend of Jeff's that Katie had met back in July. It was only at the wedding that she'd learned his last name. Roker Robertson.

"Hi, Roker." Katie waved. "What brings you out?"

"This." It was Jeff, and he raised a five-gallon propane tank.

"My fault." Roker had a sheepish look on his face. "Everyone wanted to top off their tanks before the storm, and I didn't make it here."

"But that size tank fits the grill. You want to have a cookout?" Katie sat all the way up on that one. The outside propane tank that fed the generator—and the cook stove—was the size of a refrigerator. She'd remarked on it to Jeff several times.

"I can tie it in to the generator. The hookups are exactly the same." Jeff grinned. "And if not, then sure, why not a cookout? I'll fire up the grill, and you guys can watch from inside."

"Sorry it's not more." Roker looked chagrined. "I couldn't get the propane truck out, but this will run your heater for a couple days." He looked at the oil heater sitting unused with the electricity off. "I'm guessing your water is off, too. The well pump, well, it doesn't pump very well without power."

"How did you get down the drive?" The town's propane truck was massive, and it would handle almost anything, but Roker's truck? It was in town at the city lot, and his car was an old Volvo wagon that hugged the ground.

"He's Rockhaven tough. Roker can get anywhere anytime of the year." The tank was now on the floor by the door, and Jeff had retrieved his outdoor gear from the foyer. He sat putting his heavy boots on.

"Snowshoes." Roker had his hands in his pockets.

"You didn't walk the entire way. Tell me that." She looked at Jeff hard. Roker lived two miles away. "Jeff, tell me Roker didn't walk all the way here."

"Okay. Roker didn't walk all the way here. But I bet his snowshoes did."

Roker let out a laugh, and he stifled it immediately. "Sorry, Katie."

"Oh, you people are crazy." She had moved to stand closer to the heat. "Since you're here, Roker, you two see if you can get us some power, and when you're finished, maybe we can pull the turkey from the fire."

"Yes, ma'am. I swore I smelled turkey, even from outside." Roker had a smile on his face. "That sounds pretty good to me."

"We can have pie, too." Jeff had his boots on, and he stood and stamped his feet. "Pumpkin pie."

"Don't make Roker promises. There are probably pies all over this island—" About five of them were supposed to show up that afternoon. "—but none of them are here. Sorry."

"I brought you one." Roker tilted his head sideways, rather like pointing, and he stepped to the door leading into the foyer. He returned with something wrapped in newspaper.

"How—" Katie was beside herself. Pleased, too, but totally flabbergasted. As far as she knew, the last time Roker had cooked anything, it was a wiener at the Rockhaven Town Cookout. On the end of a wire coat hanger. And he'd burned that. He was a microwave chef, not one to make pies.

"Here." He held it out to her.

"Thank you, but—"

"Roker didn't make it." Jeff interrupted her, stepping over and putting an arm around her. "Jess up on High Road did this, and when she saw Roker out, she made him bring it. It'll be good. Jess is the best pie cook on the island."

Katie's eyes teared up as she reached for the pie.

"I'm—" Roker released the wrapped pie, but he still held his hands under it. "You—not pumpkin? I didn't think, that maybe—"

"Katie?" Now Jeff was in the mix. "Are you okay?" He took the pie gently from her hands and handed it back to Roker, to give her a hug as the big man moved away, standing awkwardly with the pie still in his hands.

"I'm fine. Thank you, Roker." Katie smiled and waved him away with one hand. "Put it in the kitchen, and thank you for bringing the pie. We will all enjoy it very much."

He sauntered off, shaking his head, muttering about women and something or the other about how much easier it had been when Jeff lived on his own.

"Don't worry about him. Roker's a card, and he'll do anything for you, but that doesn't mean you'll ever understand him."

"I understand one thing." Katie had separated herself from Jeff by then. "I'm going in there and telling that man that pumpkin pie is my favorite, and I'm having two slices."

"Ho, ho! Pumpkin? I was certain it was apple." Jeff's eyes twinkled when he said that, and he reached to pull a strand of hair from her temple.

"Apple's your favorite, and when I'm with you, that makes it my favorite. When a man brings me a pumpkin pie through three feet of snow, then pumpkin's my favorite. That means you need to get with the program, Jeff Ragsdale. Today, pumpkin pie is at the top of a very short list."

"And the rest of that list?" He chuckled, but so softly it was hardly there.

"Baked turkey and electricity. I want a shower." She popped him on the shoulder. "Now, go."

"And me? I don't make the list?" He held up both hands, palms out, with a hangdog look on his face.

"If you ever get my water on. Heat, too, I could use

some of that."

"Roker?" Jeff called toward the kitchen.

"Yes?" Roker stepped into the room licking his fingers. "You ready?"

"How's the pie?" Katie slapped Roker on the shoulder as she stepped past him and into the kitchen.

"Good." He slurped one last finger. "You're not upset or nothing? About the pie, I mean?"

Katie turned to see him peering in the door. The pie was on the table, and about a fourth of it was gone. She heard Jeff in the other room, "Roker, not already. That was for lunch."

"Did I ever tell you, pumpkin is my favorite? With so much of this gone, it must indeed be the best on the island." Katie crossed her arms and leaned against the table right next to the pie. "What's your final opinion? Should I have a slice now, or wait?"

"Um—" Roker looked back at Jeff, and he turned to Katie as if not sure how to answer.

"Will you have a second slice if I have one, too?" Katie stepped to the cupboard and pulled out saucers and flatware. "Jeff, are you joining us?"

"Yes, ma'am, Dame Carver." He called it louder than absolutely necessary.

"That's settled, Roker. It's cold out there, and if you and Jeff are hooking up power, then I'm giving you food to warm you up."

Katie smiled at the big man's look of anticipation as she cut into the golden pie. She served up three slices, two large, and one that was half as big. It was Thanksgiving, the Christmas holidays were rolling in, and besides, her stomach hadn't been all it could be the last few days.

She dismissed the idea that it had been the last few mornings, thinking it would sort itself out in time. It was one of those things that came with new marriages, an attentive husband, and a perfect life.

To Katie it was about the pumpkin pie, the thick layer of snow covering the island, and the bathroom that was too cold to use. She carried her pie into the living room, and she curled up on the sofa she and Jeff had pulled up right before the fire, and she found out something.

Jess up on High Road did make the best pumpkin pies on the island. How did she know? She was holding a slice in her hand, and every single bite was even better than promised.

Either that or she was very hungry. One way or the other, Roker was the man of the hour.

She was equally pleased about ten minutes later when the lamp beside the chair came on, and the oil heater clicked three times and the fan began to run.

Then the muffled sound of running water came through the bathroom door.

"Yikes," she yelped, setting her half-finished pie aside. "The tub!"

She kicked off her blanket, and dashing in, twisted the faucet to stop the flow. She also flushed the toilet to clear the bowl from earlier. As the hand-carved wood sign above the porcelain throne said, "Yellow Is Mellow; Brown Goes Down." Apparently, on the island, conservation was the rule, and Katie tried to abide by it, even if she did sometimes think it extreme. After all, how much water could two people use?

When she returned, Jeff and Roker were in the foyer peeling outerwear loose and stamping feet. She knocked on the glass door and waved, before moving back to the sofa. When the door opened, it was Roker who spoke first.

"Getcha warmer'n a bear cub snuggled with its momma." He grinned, pointing to the heater. "It come on?"

"When the lights did. We have water, too. Showers!" She rubbed her hands together excitedly.

"No showers." Jeff leaned over the sofa to kiss her on the cheek.

"Nope. No showers with just the generator." Roker shook his head. "Cept once."

"And that means?"

Roker laughed, and Jeff looked amused. It turned out the backup generator had been here several years. Three winters before, Jeff had been off island for an extended trip, and a storm had taken out the electricity, as it had today. Roker had no backup generator, and he'd come to stay at Jeff's until repairs were done to the power lines. The second day, he'd climbed in the shower and soaped up. Then, flipping the water on, he'd waited and waited for it to warm.

Jeff interrupted Roker's story, laughing so hard he could barely talk, to tell her that his friend didn't know the water heater circuits bypassed the generator. It just pulled too much power. Roker had to shower in water that must have been about forty degrees.

She could heat water for a bath, though. That worked pretty well.

"Thanks and no thanks. I'll wait for the power to come back." Katie pulled her blanket tighter under her chin, and she stared at the flames in the fireplace.

"Sure." Jeff found the cushion beside her. "Anything you want."

Roker wasn't finished, though. "That time I was here? It was nine days. Nine days. Think I can have another piece of pie, Katie?"

She waved her hand over her shoulder to tell him to go ahead, and she turned to Jeff, mouthing, "Nine days?"

He shrugged. "It's Rockhaven. What can I say?"

Katie knew. He could say hot water, as in Boston. However, when she had Boston without Jeff, she hadn't been happy, and now, even with no hot water, she was very happy, indeed. Was it worth it being here on this crazy, snow-bound island in the middle of a storm? Absolutely, even if it was still the middle of fall.

When she reached for the rest of her pie, she found it gone. She looked around to see her plate in Roker's hands, and the rest of the pie going into his mouth.

Ah, well, she thought. I didn't need it, anyway. Any more and she would kill her appetite for lunch.

She didn't want to do that. It was Thanksgiving Day, after all, and the turkey was still in the fire.

3

"A short service tomorrow morning, starting about eleven." As she replied to her caller's question, Katie held her phone to her ear and flipped through the church directory, looking for the N's. Nickerson, Nickerson . . . finding him, she checked Bryan Nickerson off on her list.

Katie had finally decided her Saturday morning would be easier if she stayed close to the phone. Bryan wasn't the first caller. That had been Tom Schutmaat and his wife Jackie up on 4th Street. It was their week to open the church—fire up the furnace, lights on, and such—and they didn't figure it made much sense if there wasn't to be a service. They lived just down the street, they reminded Katie, so getting there wasn't too much of a problem, but there were others that would have more trouble.

As Tom said that, Katie had looked out the window at the snow that still covered everything, in spite of the fact that it was now Saturday. Even the sun, blindingly bright through the uncovered windows, hadn't melted any of it. Yeah, she'd thought. We might have trouble getting to the church. She didn't say that, though. Instead, she'd agreed with the Schutmaats' assessment of the situation and thanked them for their foresight.

Katie had decided she might as well phone the entire church body when Jeff had intervened. Oh, no, he'd laughed, flipping to the final page in the directory. He pointed to the phone tree, with the Schutmaats at the top, and branching out from there. Tom and Jackie hadn't called because they were on the schedule to open the church, but rather because they were at the top of the tree. Two people called two people, and they called two people, and so on. Pretty soon, the entire island would know, and Jeff only had to speak to one person. Neat, huh, he'd asked her, with a twinkle in his eyes.

When she'd shown him the ones who had already called her, he'd grinned as she pointed to their names at the bottom of the list. "Eager beavers," he'd said with a chuckle, giving her the short message to read out to anyone else who called. "We like eager beavers. They're the ones who show no matter what the weather does."

"Katie, we're out of eggs." That was Roker. After polishing off the turkey on Thanksgiving night, Jeff had refused to send him home. There were extra bedrooms, he'd said, and Roker knew which one was his.

"There's oatmeal in the pantry." Roker had an appetite, and Katie wasn't surprised to be out of eggs after three days with extra company in the house.

He appeared in the door with a steaming pan of scrambled eggs, stirring with a spatula. "Nah, we've got eggs for breakfast. This is just all of 'em. Jeff said he was hungry, and my cinnamon buns were gone, so I decided to throw something together. You want sausage in yours?"

"Sausage is fine." The eggs were still runny, and Katie guessed Roker had the meat already prepped to go in. He'd taken over the cooking for the weekend, so she saw no use in trying to tweak a good thing, even if the pantry was growing barer by the meal. Roker ate a lot.

"Sounds right, there." He grinned, turning back to the kitchen.

"Where's Jeff?" She realized she hadn't seen him in a while.

"You didn't know?" His head reappeared, and then his pan, and he pointed with the pan out the expanse of windows towards the water. "Down there." And he was gone again, the sound of the pan on the burner bright with his big man's heavy touch.

Sure enough. Tracks in the snow led around the house and towards the dock. There at the end, in the square box that perched high over the water, stood Jeff, attaching guy wires to the railings, one at each of the four corners of the box. In the middle was the most beautiful sight Katie thought she'd ever seen. It was a snow-covered tree, or somewhat snow covered, as it hadn't snowed since Thursday, but there it was, standing at the end of the dock, and Jeff was securing it against the upcoming season.

Christmas, the first sign it was really on the way.

The snow might have interrupted Katie's timeline for planning her holiday extravaganza, but it hadn't kept Jeff from his. He'd promised her a tree, but she didn't expect it there.

It was beautiful, though, and not just the tree. The whole scene, Jeff bundled in his heavy coat, his knit cap covering his head and ears, and the gloves on his hands. He held pliers, and he twisted wires running from the trunk of the tree to fittings at each corner of the box, tightening them repeatedly until he was satisfied.

She thought about her phone, and texting a picture to her good friend Winnie Catron back in Boston. Or New York, or wherever her latest fashion shoot was. That reminded her that her phone had to have a signal to text, and it had been dead all day. No town power; no phone signal. That was life on the island.

Then, of all things, Jeff pulled a plastic bin up beside the tree, and opening the top, he lifted enormous red bows and began to wire them to the branches. Katie felt her eyes water. That was her Jeff out there, bringing Christmas to the whole world, even though the world was snowed in, and no one would see.

"He does that every year, you know." Roker came up beside her, and he set a plate of steaming eggs on the table for her. He took his plate, mounded even higher, and he walked to the window and began to eat while watching Jeff with his red ribbons.

"Every year. That's nice." That meant it wasn't just for her. "It's pretty."

"It's more than pretty." Roker turned to her, speaking in between bites. "Those are his Katie bows. I call it his Katie tree."

Katie stood and walked to the window to stand beside Roker. Katie bows? Jeff had two of them in his hands, and he ducked under one of the guy wires, to disappear on the opposite side of the tree. It moved, telling that he was attaching the bows to branches on the opposite side.

"Katie bows," she murmured, reaching to put her fingers on the glass. "That might need some explaining."

"Oh, easy." Roker scraped the final eggs into his mouth and chewed once before swallowing them. He pointed out the window with his fork. "One for each Christmas. He said he didn't care how big a tree he had to get, he was adding another ribbon for you every year."

Katie laughed. "That might be a really big tree someday."

"Oh, no." Roker was on the way back to the kitchen. "That's all the ribbons. He won't add any more."

"No more?" Easy to explain? Katie smiled. Roker had only confused her more.

"Yeah," he called from the kitchen. "Every year you weren't here he added a ribbon. The first year there was only one, and the tree was about two feet tall. He called them his Katie promises, and he wanted the whole island to know you were coming back some day." He could be heard laughing. "I'm glad you came back when you did. Pretty soon, we wouldn't be able to get the tree on the dock."

Katie felt her heart expand watching that man out there in the snow, doing something he always did, just because it was what he did, and the thing was, he'd been doing it all along for her, even when she hadn't been here to notice.

That meant one thing and one thing only. This Christmas had to be the best one ever. The biggest tree, the best decorations, and the finest gifts she had ever put together. She could get the whole church family involved, maybe even plan a bash at the Town Hall. Invite the whole island!

Gumdrops and candy canes swam in Katie's eyes as she pictured a flotilla of Christmas boats moored in the cove, all arriving in their holiday best, greeted by a fully garbed Santa out on the float.

"Roker," she called loudly. "How do you like the color red?"

"Red?"

"Yes, red." She turned and he was at the kitchen door, wiping his hands with a towel, his sleeves rolled up past his wrists. It looked like he'd been washing dishes.

"Don't know. Never thought about it."

"You need to start." Katie smiled. She'd not noticed before, but he was wearing red plaid flannel. For warmth, probably, but it certainly fit the season. "Lots of red, and white."

"Red and white," almost as if he'd never considered the two colors as compatible. He shrugged as he turned back to the kitchen, continuing, "Sure, I like red and white, though don't know why anyone would put the two together."

Santa Claus, Katie mused, looking back towards the dock, to see the tree finished and Jeff missing.

"Red and white?" Strong arms, warm with exertion, encircled her.

"I didn't notice you coming in." Katie pulled the arms tighter, smelling the remains of outside on her man.

"My boots were a mess, and I used the mudroom. What's this about red and white? Are we redecorating?"

"Roker, maybe." She smiled at that.

"Does he know?" He chuckled. "Visit his house, sometime. I'm not sure it's ever been decorated."

"Not his house, just Roker. The tree. It's pretty. Tell me about it."

Katie wanted to hear the story in Jeff's words. However, just then, a cardinal landed on a tree just up from the shore, disturbing the snow still mounded on one of the branches. The white powder dissipated into a cloud of haze, creating a cascading effect as it tumbled earthward, the effect growing more pronounced as more branches shed their cotton candy bounty.

The red bird took to wing, startled by the sudden movement; and brilliant against the white background, it made its way to the Katie Tree, landing on a small branch at the top. It bobbed a few times as the branch absorbed its weight, but with Jeff having moved it that morning, the majority of the snow was gone, and the bird seemed content.

"Bird, go away," Jeff whispered in her ear.

"No. It's pretty." To Katie, it was like a living Katie bow, a red symbol of how much Jeff must have loved her all those years she was away, and how much that meant he loved her now. "Don't ever tell it to go away."

"Okay, Dame Carver. On one condition." His face rested next to hers, and he watched out the window. However, he didn't go on.

"I give." Katie started to look at Jeff, but his face was so close, she only brushed cheek to cheek. She smiled, instead. "Just name it."

"That you spend every Christmas with me for the rest of your life."

She laughed. She got it, what Jeff wasn't really saying. It was the ribbons, one for each Christmas they'd been apart. The cardinal—very much like one of the red decorations—meant a missed Christmas. Katie had seen only the beauty, but Jeff had seen something else. He'd seen the years he'd spent wishing for her to return.

"Thank you for the tree. It's beautiful. Is it beautiful to you?"

"Of course. Every bow is a reminder of the woman I adore."

Katie was so in love she thought she would cry.

"Hey, you two. You gonna stand there gaping at

that tree all day?" It was Roker, and his voice was loud. It carried a measure of excitement, too.

"Might." Jeff didn't move, but continued to hold Katie tightly.

"Just that out front, thought I saw something that might interest you two. I told Katie, already. We're out of eggs."

"Out of eggs," Jeff whispered, snorting. He called louder, "And that means?"

"Certain it was the plow. Bet we could get out, now."

It was something they'd been expecting all weekend, the plow. Without it, no one would be at church the following morning. There was still the drive to consider, though. The town snowplow didn't do residential drives, and Jeff and Katie's was a winding twist through towering spruce. The snow was there until they cleared it themselves.

And Roker seeing the plow? He must have been keeping an eye out. The road was barely visible in winter, and not at all in summer.

"Driveway. Not plowed." Jeff called it, but not loudly.

"Jeep. If it'll mud bog, it'll plow snow." Katie disengaged Jeff's arms. "Roker's right. We're running low on food. We should get to town today."

"And take Roker home." Jeff put his hands in his pockets and nodded his head his friend's way. "Catch that, Roker?"

"Hadn't thought of that. My own bed sounds good." He frowned as if considering, then he nodded with a smile. "Have to visit the store, first. Then, maybe I can get the town truck down to refill your tank."

It was good he thought of that, because just then, the lights flickered, the oil heater went silent, and the only sound in the house was the crackling of the wood in the fireplace.

"Don't touch the oven," Roker called out, already back in the kitchen, with the sound of things rattling around. "Maybe my new batch of rolls will cook anyway. At least we still have water."

That enthusiasm ended about five minutes later with the sputtering of water from the pipes.

What had Roker said? Nine days? It seemed that if they had the plows clearing the street, surely they could get the power lines back in operation. Katie wanted her shower, and she wanted it now.

"Katie? Going with us?" It was Jeff, and he held the keys in his hand.

It was heading out the door when Katie knew everything would work out perfectly. There, sitting on the hood of the Jeep, brilliant against the mounded snow, was her Katie cardinal, a reminder to her that love had brought her to her island, and it was love that made everything okay.

Even Roker showering her with snow as he cleared the windows couldn't take that away. After all, it was almost Christmas!

Ring the bells, she wanted to sing, but when she climbed inside, she also wanted the heat on high, and she made sure both men knew just how cold the seat really was.

4

"I see you're stocking up, Mrs. Ragsdale."

"You know, with the snow . . ." Katie smiled, not finishing her sentence, and nodding at the thin, white-haired cashier, as she began to unload her cart at the checkout stand. Her battered nametag identified her as Ada Parkes, but Katie knew she was known about Rockhaven as Ada Simpers. Mr. Simpers had been here and gone, a late in life name-change for the cashier that had outlasted the man she married.

The grocery store was better stocked than Katie had expected despite the weather that had kept them penned in the house for two days. She hadn't thought it through, that while they were penned, maybe everyone wasn't. The town roads were perfectly clear—and dry—from the school down Main and past the ferry landing. It wasn't until she thought about it that she realized she hadn't heard the ferry all weekend, but only because she'd stayed inside the entire time.

That's cold weather, for you, she mused. Windows were for summer, and in summer, you heard everything. She would get used to the change, but now she was shopping, and Jeff was delivering Roker to his house. She hoped he didn't get stuck there, and leave her here.

She pushed the last of her things forward, including eggs and a large can of pumpkin filling, as the cashier began totaling her bill, one item at a time.

"Ah, and you and the new man out there on the Cove. Moffat's never been easy in bad weather." The eggs went under the scanner, two cartons, eighteen in each. "When Mrs. Ragsdale—your man's mother—was alive, in weather like this, they came to town. Course, they heated with wood, then. Now you have a good oil stove, and you're toasty as a mouse. Wouldn't take for mine, not on a cold Rockhaven night."

"When it works." Katie pushed her bread forward, making it easier to reach. "Oh, and can I get you to add a tank of propane? I'll get it on the way out."

"Certainly. Two-and-a-half or five?" Gallons, she meant, but that went without saying, and Katie understood it as such.

"Five. Can I bring in the empty one tomorrow?" Katie thought the one Roker had supplied was a five. If not, then she'd settle that later.

"Not tomorrow." The cashier's eyes twinkled as she smiled, and she reached to touch Katie on the arm. "Not open on Sunday."

"Monday, then, unless you have to have it today."

"I've put the deposit here." She pulled the receipt from the register and spread it out for Katie, and she pointed. "You bring this back with your empty, and we'll get you a refund. I'm sorry I don't have anyone to help you to your car. The eldest Peavey was to come in for a few hours today, but there's just me."

"I've got Jeff here. He just ran down the street. Thank you, Mrs. Simpers."

"Don't you get chilled out there. The sun's pretty, but it's not warm by any measure."

"I'll wait just inside." Katie pointed to the vestibule of the store, separated by glass doors from the inside. It was where the carts were kept. "You have a really good day."

"Thank you, dear. I usually do." Mrs. Simpers smiled and stepped into the store, disappearing among the shelves of merchandise.

The inside doors were automatic, and they slipped aside as Katie approached with her cart. It was colder in the vestibule, and she pulled her gloves from her bag and slipped them on. Glancing up, she looked at the vent and wondered if it was disconnected. About then, it began to whistle, settling to a gentle vibration as the heating system kicked on. She felt the warmth wash her face, and it felt good. However, after only a minute, it kicked off.

"So much for that," she muttered, pulling her collar higher against her neck.

A truck drove by just in front of the store, and it turned into the town lot across the street. A big man, bundled against the cold, got out and went into a wood-shingled building just to the side. Katie tried to remember what was in that building. A sign was beside the door, but at the angle she couldn't read it. After a few minutes he came out, carrying something flat, and climbed back in his truck, his lights flashing, and pulled into the street. He stopped in front of an empty building just past the Post Office, took the flat object inside, and in minutes, his lights flashed again, and he was gone. There was no one else.

The sun caught on the water in the harbor. It was greeting card perfect, with the houses built right up to the shore, the brightly colored doors and shutters, and the roofs mounded with snow. Several had smoke coming from chimneys, but even more were shuttered, closed up for the season. Water was drained, heaters were off, and furniture was covered to keep eight months of dust from invading the summer fabrics. It was nearly a ghost town, but what a beautiful ghost town! With the storm, Rockhaven had become a snow-covered wonderland paradise, as stunning a location to live as any in the world.

She caught the buzz of the glass, and reaching to crack one of the doors, she heard the faintest sound of a ferry horn. She smiled at that. Island ferries were like the Post Office. Neither rain, snow, nor sleet, except that in case of the ferry, high winds could indeed park the ship. After a moment, she saw it come around the headland at the harbor entrance, and she laughed. There was one car on board. All that distance, over an hour of travel, and one car had come to the island.

Probably none would return. Yet, the ferry would run anyway. What could she say? It was Rockhaven.

A horn honked, and Katie looked the other direction. It was Jeff, in his green Jeep, and he waved through his opened window. He was pulled up at the Post Office just next door. She waved back, not sure he could see her, and she pulled her hood around her face, ready to push her cart out the door. By the time she had begun to move forward, he was out and to the door, and pulling it open.

"Brr, Katie! Cold!" He pulled the door to behind him, and he rubbed his hands together, blowing on them. "Did they have everything you needed?"

"Eggs, in case Roker comes back." She laughed, lifting the bag with the two cartons inside. "Eighteens, two of them."

"Heard Kevie might be here. Thought we could offer him a way home if he is." He peered inside, waving. "I see Ada didn't let the weather keep her away. Let me check."

"Jeff—" He'd already started that direction, and Katie called to stop him. "—he's not here. Mrs. Simpers said he didn't show today."

"No? Blame the weather." The doors had already opened, and he called inside to Mrs. Simpers, "No, don't need a thing. How's business today?"

Katie didn't catch what was being said on the other side of the conversation, but it probably went much like hers had. She bumped Jeff with her cart, and when he looked, she motioned with her head that it was time to get moving. "It's cold out here."

"You stay warm, Mrs. Simpers," he called, as he stepped back to let the doors slide shut. "You roll, and I'll start the car. You can warm up while I load. How's that?"

He was already moving, and Katie pushed the cart forward. Outside, she realized the heat had been on in the vestibule. It was thirty degrees colder outside. Once inside the Jeep, she turned the heat on high and held her gloves in front of the vents.

When Jeff joined her, she grabbed his bare wrist with her hand. "Freezing out there. Did you get the propane? I paid for it, already."

"In the back. Roker should be finished by the time we're home, though. It'll be good to have a spare, just in case. Colder'n Boston?" He grinned like he already knew the answer to that.

"Let's just say Rudolph would be at home here."

"Wait until February. This is a walk in the park compared." He had his gloves off and his hands in front of the vents, too. "Notice the empty store? It's not going to be empty for long." He pointed to the large building just the other side of the Post Office. It had plate glass windows, and there was a big red SALE PENDING sign in the left-hand one.

"I saw the sign going in. New restaurant? Or clothes, maybe." She hadn't realized it was the sign, but it must have been what the man carried. She wouldn't mind that. And, it seemed to her it was a good location to catch the tourist season ferry traffic.

"Never can tell. They've got six months to remodel, just in time for the summer rush. Bet you were already thinking that." He grinned, and with one foot pushing in the clutch, he grabbed the wheel and the shift lever, and he eased it into gear and backed into the street.

"I heard your family used to winter in town." Katie hadn't paid Mrs. Simpers' comment much attention, but here, in the car, and with no one around and no place, really, to go, it came to her.

"Ha!" He laughed a short and emphatic bark of a sound. "She can call it wintering. Where to? Lunch, if anything's open?"

"You skipped right off that question. And, do you think anything's open?" It had been several hours since her eggs, and the donuts in the back? She had a craving, already, and she needed to kill it with real food. She was distracted by the buzzing of a small airplane overhead. She watched it head west. There was a landing field out towards the back side of the island.

Jeff looked up at the noise. "Surprised someone's coming in on a day like this. Must be staying at one of the big houses, possibly until Christmas."

"How nice for them, but we're talking about food."

"Right, right. Harbor View, maybe. They never close, if they're home. Today, if you didn't see them get on the ferry, they're home. I can check, though." It was the other way, and he did a tight u-turn in the street.

"You're sure? Never?"

"They live above the store. How can they close? The restaurant kitchen is their kitchen." He gave the engine gas, safe on the dry street, and two seconds later, he hit the brakes, and pulled up parallel to Harbor View. The sign on the door said closed. "See? A light's on inside."

"It says they're closed. Can't you read?" Katie flipped the blind down on her side, and she twisted her back to the door. "You, though, I want to know where your family stayed in town. Mrs. Simpers was very clear. In bad weather, she said your mother came to town. Where did you stay?"

"Okay, if you must hear the story. My momma stayed in town, not my dad and me."

"You stayed . . . at the house? Why?"

"Look in the harbor."

"Sure." Katie glanced out, and it seemed very much like it had from the store windows.

"Where's Chipper's boat? And Rod's, and while you're at it, look for Al's and Winer's." He had a grin on his face as he spoke.

Katie shrugged. "At home?" She didn't know those men's boats well enough to recognize them, except maybe Al's, and that was if she saw Al on it at his dock. And it occurred to her that Al kept his boat in town, like most of the island fishermen. Jeff was lucky to have a permanent mooring in Moffat Cove, and she'd never thought of it that way.

"A day like this, they're out hauling pots."

"You're telling me you and your dad stayed at your house and went fishing?" Fishing! Wrong word! "Sorry. Lobstering."

"You knew dad. He was a die-hard. That's why I don't lobster in weather like this." He looked to something behind Katie.

Katie jumped at the sound of knuckles rapping on the glass. Turning, she saw Nina Vinson, the proprietor at the shop. She rolled the window down, and she felt her skin cut by the sharpness of the cold. "Yes?"

"Saw you two out here, and I thought you might want lunch. You headed inside?" She was in a sweater, and she stamped her feet, rubbing her hands together and shaking her head. "Sorry, trying to warm up."

"If you're open—" Katie began, hesitantly.

"Girl, we're always open. Come on in." Nina patted Katie on the shoulder, and still rubbing her hands, she high-stepped back across the snow-covered sidewalk and into the building.

"Told you." Jeff had a broad smile on his face.

"But . . ." Katie laughed to herself. "It says closed. Why not turn the sign around?"

"No need. Everyone knows." Jeff was pulling his gloves on. "Ready?"

"How does everyone know?" She didn't, and she was someone.

"Just like everyone knows about my tree on my dock, and what those ribbons mean. It's Rockhaven. No secrets on the rock." He leaned forward and gave her a short kiss on the lips. "That's how they all knew you were coming back to the island."

"I wasn't here to tell them. They couldn't know that. I didn't even know, not for fourteen years." Katie shook her head, pulling her own gloves on.

"I knew it. Now, let's have lunch, just not lobster. I get that on my boat every day." He flipped his door open, and he climbed from the car.

Katie remembered what he'd told her that July day outside the church when she'd been so upset at the entire town knowing she was back, certain he had convinced them that she and Jeff might still be in love. *If I had said nothing about you, these people still would have known.*

Okay, she thought. I haven't started putting together Christmas yet, and I wonder who knows what I'm planning?

It was Kent Vinson, already at the grill, who called out to her, "I hear you're dressing Roker as Santa this year? Thought I'd never see the day!" And he burst into riotous laughter, standing there with breaded steak in his hand, waiting to toss it on the fire.

Katie put her hands on her hips, prepared to glare at Jeff, but when she turned to him, he had his hands up and a puzzled look on his face.

Katie started to laugh. She guessed Jeff was right, at least about this. Then, if Kent knew that, he certainly knew how much she loved Jeff, so she threw her arms around him and kissed him firmly on the mouth.

"Oh, get a room," Kent called, as the sizzle of the steak carried into the room.

Katie waved one hand at him and ignored him. They had a whole house, but it wasn't here, and Jeff was.

"Whew," he said, when she released him. "What was that for?"

"Some secrets I want the world to know. This way they don't have to guess."

"Then they'd better know my secrets, too," and he kissed her back, right in front of Nina and Kent and anyone who happened to be looking inside. The windows, fogged with the season's snows, told the true story. A fairy tale romance was happening just inside the door of this ordinary building, and if no one believed it, just look across the island. It was God's Christmas icing on the magical land of Rockhaven, where every kiss brought peace and goodwill into the hearts of men.

In this case, into Jeff and Katie's hearts, but in that kiss, theirs were the only ones that counted.

They were in love, and Christmas was only weeks away. What a lovely Christmas it would be!

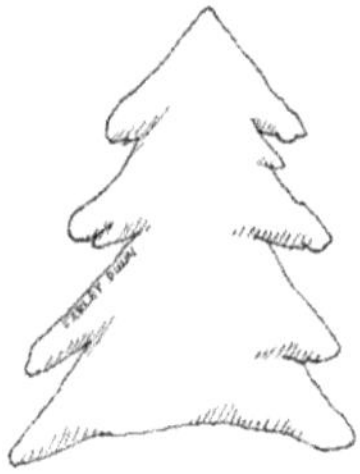

5

The service that Sunday morning was sparsely attended. Katie felt a sense of disappointment that Jeff's preparations were only for a couple handfuls of people. It was Sunday, she thought, as she lifted her voice to recite the Lord's Prayer. What else do island people have to do when the whole place is snowed under?

Still, those that had braved the roads, ones that while plowed, weren't really completely clear, were bright and friendly, as if they had been apart for weeks, and were renewing old friendships. Bryan Nickerson was one of the first to show, and Kent and Nina, telling Katie that they were welcome to come by for lunch. They'd be open, and Nina had flashed her a quick grin. Al, Janine, and the boys had bustled in just as the service started.

Tom and Jackie were of course there before anyone else. Gracious people, they'd held the door for Jeff and Katie.

"Sorry we didn't get the walks," Tom had apologized. "Trying to get my own done, and the old ticker, it doesn't tick as strong as it used to. Getting up in years, you know." He'd tapped his chest and chuckled, but his cheeks were red, and it was clear he'd done enough.

Jackie had pulled him away, after giving Katie a hug, murmuring that Tom "should leave the minister alone to prepare for the morning."

The air in the auditorium was warm, although the walls emanated a chill that told of an unheated building over the course of the night. Even the benches had yet to warm. The mid-morning sun through the colored windows shimmered across the interior, and Katie was glad Jeff had decided to open the church even with the remains of the storm filling driveways and back roads; and the people who might choose to let those obstacles keep them away.

She remembered Jeff's "eager beavers," and she smiled. Even without looking, she was certain she could name everyone sitting in the benches this morning. As Jeff walked to the dais and spread his things before him, she pulled out her tablet and opened it. She had been pleased to learn church members were encouraged to use electronic devices for note taking and to access the most current online Bibles. She clicked hers on, prepared to take detailed notes over the service. As the minister's wife she made it her duty to send them to her list of missing parishioners, those either unable to attend due to weather or other circumstances, or the summer people who called the church their home just during the warm months of the year.

This one, of course, would go out before she left the church. She had a signal here on the building's Wi-Fi, but at home, with town power still off, there was nothing.

Scrolling her list of email addresses, one stood out to her. Ritchey Hickox, Jeff's good friend from all those years ago. Her friend, too, she guessed, although Ritchey had been an island boy, in contrast to Katie's summer status. Now it was reversed. Katie was the island girl, and Ritchey was nowhere to be found.

To be more specific, Ritchey was somewhere, just that Texas was pretty nowhere when you were on a Maine island in the middle of winter. In Texas, in November, they were probably still in shorts and Tees, unlike here with frozen pipes and water heaters that didn't work. Visiting the motel for a shower was sounding pretty good to Katie. She'd heated water for a bath, one heavy lobster pot at a time, but it hadn't been all that warm, and it had cooled fast.

Something Jeff said caught her attention, and she looked to him and smiled. He was down front presenting the children's message, and the youngest three Peavey boys were among the handful of children whose parents had braved their snow-filled drives this weekend. One of them, Karlton, she thought, although their backs were to her, and she couldn't really see, laughed out loud at part of the story. The adults scattered throughout the audience laughed with him.

Jeff was so good with kids, to have none of his own. He would make a fine parent, someday.

Glancing back down, she clicked on Ritchey's name, and the replies he'd made over the past six weeks appeared. After moving onto the island, she'd found him on Facebook, and she'd brought him up to date on Jeff and their life on the island, and asked why she hadn't seen him at the wedding.

It seemed his third child had come at the end of September—three weeks early—and they'd had to cancel their plans. When she'd asked Jeff about it, he'd brushed it off as unimportant, telling Katie that Ritchey had let him know the situation, and he understood. Katie had known better. It was what Jeff hadn't said, and the look of resignation on his face, that told the real answer he couldn't say.

She'd also read between Ritchey's words in the email: his wife, and his kids, and how much trouble the trip would be for her. Not for Ritchey, but for her. And how she needed him at home. Even a weekend was too long for him to be gone.

Now Ritchey sent her a short reply each week, a thank you or something humorous about someone she'd mentioned in the week's sermon notes.

Christmas. Ritchey and Christmas. That would be something to pull together, if only she could figure out how.

Katie watched Jeff stand, and she idly tapped her tablet on the edge, ready to start her notes on the morning service, as the handful of children made their way back to their scattered parents. She would include

Jeff's outline, of course, but her more personal narrative would make the people feel as if they were actually here.

She tapped the darkened screen to wake it, and she began her first line:

"Sunday morning, Thanksgiving weekend, Jeff Ragsdale speaking.

"Jeff calls children to the front; tells story of the Wise Men; Karlton Peavey laughs, and the church finds it humorous.

"Jeff sends the children to their parents and begins his message . . ."

All Katie had to do here was insert Jeff's sermon notes, and she clicked and pasted them in. Now she had a break until he began to wind things down. It was visiting speakers that kept her fingers busy the entire service. She had to take down the core points in everything they said.

As she set the tablet on the bench at her side, it softly dinged. Looking at it, she noted a new email from Winnie. In her preview window, it showed, "Hey, Sweetie, I'm not at church this morning . . ."

Katie growled beneath her breath, and she picked up the device and tapped a hurried and somewhat irritated reply. "I'm ashamed of you. Get to church!" and she hit Send.

The reply was almost immediate. "I can't. I'm babysitting. And the baby is so cute . . ."

The emails were still in preview mode, and Katie clicked to bring them up. The full text didn't give her much more information. The messages were very short. That meant Winnie was leading her on. Besides, who did her friend know that had kids she could babysit? No one that Katie was aware of.

"Whose baby?" She typed it and hit Send. Then, immediately, she sent another email, "Where are you?"

The reply was one word. "Texas."

"And?" Katie hit Send again. Texas was a big state. It could be almost anywhere. She remembered Winnie's Colorado photo shoot, and refrained from rolling her eyes. Maybe she had been called back out West, the ideal cowgirl. She sent, "Modeling?"

It was two minutes this time before she saw her reply. "Sorry. The baby. To answer you, not today, Sweetie. Babies are so cute. You need one. I've got a feeding, so I'll talk to you later. Don't forget you've got a phone, and it accepts text messages. Turn it on sometime."

This time Katie did roll her eyes, and when she heard Jeff stumble over a Greek phrase he was pronouncing with some difficulty, she looked to see him with a puzzled expression on his face. His eyes were on her. She smiled and waved to let him know all was fine. She pulled her phone from her purse, and held it just above the bench to show him what the problem was.

He nodded and began the difficult-to-pronounce phrase again.

Katie let the series of emails scroll through her thoughts. Winnie, Texas, and a baby. Somehow, she couldn't put the three together. There was no common cord there at all.

Her phone vibrated in her hand, and she glanced down to see the text message icon. It had the number fourteen on it.

Fourteen text messages? Good heavens! What was that about? She unlocked the phone and tapped the icon. The last one pulled up first.

"Now, Sweetie, does it all make sense?"

Katie scrolled up. All fourteen were from Winnie. She'd been sending all weekend, and only now that her phone had synced with the church Wi-Fi was it catching up.

After reading through them, she sent one in reply. "How do you know Ritchey Hickox?"

It seemed Winnie was at his house in Houston. Ritchey now owned a sporting goods store with locations in Colorado Springs, Houston, and soon to come to North Carolina, just outside Raleigh. His had been the photo shoot in Colorado Winnie had attended just before Katie's and Jeff's wedding at the first of October. Of course, Winnie hadn't known that, but he'd wanted her back for a second session, this time to do a live promotion in his Houston store. He said she was perfect, she'd typed with exclamation points. They were about to expand, and he wanted Winnie to be the face of his new product line.

Still. How in the world could her friend have made this connection, and be babysitting for the very man who'd missed hers and Jeff's wedding?

The answer popped up. "Facebook." After a moment, another message appeared. "After the wedding, I looked up all Jeff's old friend, and I friended 'im. That's why Ritchey called me back, because I'm Jeff's friend, too. How 'bout that?" There was a smiley face at the end.

Katie smiled. She'd find out more of the story later, but now at least her quest from earlier didn't seem quite so impossible. Ritchey and Christmas. She might have to twist Winnie's arm to get Ritchey here, but Katie thought she now had a plan.

6

"Where did the snow go?"

Katie asked the question of no one as she stood high on the Point and pulled her sweater tighter around her neck. She had hoped to find the Point covered in Christmas icing, something she had never seen. It was still December, after all. Yet, here she stood in a sweater, so she should have expected it. Indian Summer, she believed they called it down in Massachusetts, although here in Maine, they were lucky to get one day.

Now? It was the midday sun that felt good, not the breeze blowing in off the water. Still, with much of the previous week's storm quickly disappearing, they'd been able to drive out for a picnic.

What had Katie told Janine? I need a break, and your boys need to stretch their legs. It had surprised her how fast her friend had agreed, and now they were having a picnic on the Point, and everyone was soaking up the warmth.

The day was not quite perfect, though. The road out had been a mess, with shaded areas still thick with snow, and the places that had melted? They were a muddy mess. And now, the boys were out along the shore path. Little of the snow had melted there, and Katie could just see them having a snowball fight. At least they were giving their mother some peace, and with all the boats locked in the boathouse, they couldn't get on the water.

She turned her attention from them, relieved about one thing. Being on an island, even if you ignored them, they couldn't get lost, could they? After all, it was an island.

Katie smiled.

They'd set up the picnic near the foundations of her grandmother's old summer home. It was sunny here. However, they'd brought fuel for the generator at the cabin down on the water, and even from here, Katie could hear it humming just at the edge of perception. Someone else might think it a distant boat or a plane, but she had slept a week last summer with it just outside her window, and the sound had become Jeff, or rather, his concern for her welfare. It was a good memory.

Now, it was running a small heater, and Janine was taking a well-deserved nap. Ten minutes, she had asked Katie. Give me ten minutes of peace, and I can make it until spring. It had been forty-five, and Katie had no intention of waking her yet.

It was Christmas that kept Katie wound up, or her thwarted plans for Christmas, anyway. She'd imagined lights down Jeff's drive, and two trees in the house. One at the church, of course, and manger scenes. Plural. One had to be live, in the gazebo at the Town Park. She was the minister's wife, and she could call on all the townspeople to "step up to the plate" to do this for Jeff.

She hadn't considered Rockhaven. Maine. An island fifteen miles out to sea. Storms. Ordinary island stuff like that. Unlike Boston where storms happened, the sidewalks were cleared, and life went on as usual, in Maine, a storm happened, and life shut down for three days. The Thanksgiving blizzard was proof of that.

Even the Thanksgiving dinner she had organized with her church members had been swallowed in a barrage of snow, buried three feet deep. Their only guest had been Roker, and he'd stayed the entire weekend.

Still, giant balls on the evergreen in the park. Plastic, not glass, not after the storm over the weekend. And tinsel, wired on with pliers. She'd gotten that from watching Jeff at the house. You wire stuff on, because otherwise, the wind takes it off. She could get Kevie and some of his friends to help with that.

The banquet at the Town Hall? That was proving more difficult. Corrine at the bakery said she was swamped with orders at the school. She did the treats for every class party, and of course they had them on the same day. After school was out for the holidays, thirty-four pies were already ordered, two birthday cakes always came the third week in December, and her daily cinnamon buns? She just couldn't find the time, with her daughter heading to Florida for the holiday with her grandparents from off-island.

Jess Tambour up on High Road had promised several pumpkin pies, if Katie'd clean the pumpkins—fresh, the only way to make pies—and while grateful, Katie considered it another mess she'd unwarily gotten herself into. She couldn't back out after asking, could she? Jess was a member of the church.

It crossed her mind that her friends from ALDMass would be drawing for Secret Santa about now. Gifts would start to show up on desks, and the Christmas party would line up on the 20th or the 21st, close to Christmas, but early enough for those traveling out of town to be able to attend. Last year it had been at Deuxave. Too elegant, they'd all exclaimed, but they'd had a great time nonetheless. This year, who knew?

Her desk. Who would receive their daily Christmas surprises there? Or was it empty, still? That was a bit of an emotional hollow spot, still, this being her first Christmas gone. Once she got past this one, though, she'd be fine. Surely she'd be fine.

Katie pushed that aside, moving on. Ritchey Hickox. He was proving to be a booger. Still, she was working on it. Winnie's help? Not as empowering as Katie had hoped. Come to find out, the children's nanny was babysitting, and Winnie was doing no more than pretending to give them a bit of her time. She was waiting on Ritchey to drop her off at the airport. Flights had been cancelled at Hobby Airport, closer to the Hickox's home, and she'd had to wait to be re-scheduled into Houston's larger Bush Intercontinental.

Katie had told Winnie that the two weeks of the holidays were hers. She expected her friend to be on the island the entire time. If any modeling gigs came up, she had to tell them no.

"Even Hawaii?" Winnie had teased over the phone.

"You'd better not," Katie snapped back.

"Just as well," Winnie had returned, her voice light and bright, as if there was more she wasn't saying, and Katie had played into her hands.

"Why do you say that?" Katie had been on the verge of apologizing, recognizing her inconsiderate response even as she spoke it. Being here with Jeff was the end-all dream she'd known it would be, but there was more to life than just Jeff. Getting married wasn't like doing your nails. Just clip off the old parts, and flush them down the drain. No, the life Katie had lived for twenty-eight years had to be filed gently, pampered, and polished into something that was new and comfortable. At times, she missed what she'd left behind. She missed Winnie, and she wanted to see her again.

"Oh," and Winnie was silent for a moment, with just the tapping of a pen on a desk, or so it sounded. "I already turned three down. Did you know they don't celebrate Christmas in the Maldives? How sad is that? It's just another day, shooting pictures on the beach."

"You—" and Katie heard her voice stumble. "You

turned down the Maldives in December?"

"Sweetie, I'm spending Christmas with you." Then she'd giggled. "And Jeffie, of course. How fun is this going to be? You do have an extra room, I hope. Not the sofa, please." She'd giggled again.

Ritchey, though. She had to find a connection that would be strong enough to get him here.

Connection! Katie pulled out her phone and opened the voicemail app. She tapped the microphone icon and said, "Remember to call Cousin Nikki. She might want to see Rockhaven in the dead of winter."

On second thought, really? Katie considered the plausibility of her cousin actually coming all the way to the island, but she might. With Francois to drive her, she might be willing to travel almost anywhere. Then, Katie could find out what her sole-surviving and very wealthy European relation had been up to, living in Katie's old apartment back in Boston.

Katie turned to see Janine on the deck outside the cabin. She had her jacket in her hand, and she yawned. When she saw Katie she waved.

"Where are the boys?"

"Out." Katie waved one hand toward the water. "How was your nap?"

"How long—?" She looked at her wrist and shook it. "You let me sleep an hour?"

Katie smiled and held up a finger. It was a good ways to the cabin, and she headed that direction. Yelling at each other—and they'd been pretty close to doing that—didn't make for much of a conversation. Closer, she started again.

"I thought you deserved a few minutes with someone else watching the boys. They've been fine." Katie's last comment was to forestall the frown on her friend's face at the words *someone else watching the boys.* She understood, though remembering Kevie stealing . . . no, borrowing Katie's little dinghy back in the summer, then Konnar being tossed in the ocean—twice!—by his brothers on a chilly September night. "They've been down on the shore path tossing snowballs at each other."

"Oh, my heavens!" Janine's hand went to her mouth. "Did you see Kevie putting rocks in any of them? Kevie always puts rocks in his snowballs. Kevie!" She yelled, already striding up the hill.

Getting a live nativity going in the town gazebo? A Christmas banquet for the entire town? How about getting Winnie, Nikki, and Ritchey here for the holidays? How hard could it be? If Janine could survive her four boys, Katie could do anything she dreamed up.

"Austie?" Katie called out another of hers and Jeff's summer friends from so long ago, turning and speaking to the trees as she did so, talking to no one, with Janine already gone over the rise. "Apple? Bennie and Bobby? Maybe Babes would like to come, with her new baby, even if it would be fifteen by now."

Katie got pulled away from her fanciful and carefree rhetoric with the sound of Janine's voice coming down the rise.

"Katie? Do you have the keys? We have to get to the hospital now!"

"It's Christmas, God," Katie said, although not too

loudly, as she started to run up the slope. “Can’t you be here just for Christmas, taking care of things?”

And when you show up, bring Ritchey for Jeff, and make everything else work out, too. That was all she had time to pray, because by then, they were in the car, and speeding down the driveway as fast as the rutted mud would allow.

7

Three stitches. The rock-infused snowball had hit Konnar, the nine-year-old, just on the temple, and the blood had been worse than the cut. Katie was glad for that. She hadn't been to the hospital since arriving back on the island, but in Boston it would be called an emergency clinic. There wasn't even a doctor on call. They were all in Wells or Camden or on Deer Isle. The medical technicians had been skilled, though, and the cut was repaired and bandaged, quick as a spring snowstorm melts under the warmth of the midday sun.

She wondered how it was done delivering babies on such a remote island. The thought had never occurred to her before. She might have to deal with that question someday. She made a mental note to check to see if midwifery was still a legitimate occupation.

She had called Jeff on the way to the hospital, but

he was out on his boat for the day, and voicemail had picked up her call. When Janine had rung up Al, it was the same. On the island, Katie was learning, you did for yourself, because there was no one else to do for you.

The hardest part of the drive in from the Point? The youngest Peavey, Keithie, at only four, had screamed the entire way in, with tears running down his face, convinced that his brother was going to die. Kevie, who had done the deed, had sat in the rear seat and sulked.

Maybe she didn't need to worry about midwifery services on the island, not with Janine's examples of why kids weren't a good idea. Katie was pretty sure she wasn't having one before she was forty, if then.

Now, Janine was at home with her three youngest, and Katie had Kevie riding in the car with her.

"Why do I have to go back?" Kevie had one elbow on the armrest, and his chin in his hand. His eyes were glued to the window at his side, and they narrowed at the passing scenery.

"Because I need your help." Katie said the words brightly. The real reason was Janine had been at her wit's end with the three youngest. This one had been torturing Keithie by the time Katie had driven up to their home, that Konnar was probably going to die and come back to haunt him. When Janine started to cry, Katie had stepped in and told Kevie to get in the car. They had stuff to collect at the Point.

"I've already been out there once, today. It's boring."

Katie ignored that, glad they were in Jeff's Jeep. How had she ever thought she could get Kevie to help out with her Christmas tree? He was a monster. He'd just as soon cut all the branches off, just to create trouble for someone else.

"It's Christmas in three weeks." Okay, Katie thought to herself. Where am I going with that?

"What's special about that?" Kevie threw himself back into the seat, crossing his arms across his chest.

"Kevie, how can you say that?" Katie downshifted the transmission going up an incline, and she glanced at him. He wasn't a bad-looking kid, stocky, with even features. Just to see him you wouldn't think him anything but adorable. It was when he moved or spoke that the real boy came out. But to not like Christmas?

"It's not real. None of it."

That was too much for Katie, and she pulled the car to the side of the road and set the parking brake. She reached and turned the key, killing the engine.

"What? Am I in trouble for telling the truth?" Kevie snorted and refused to look at her. He had his knuckles at the glass, and he rapped it repeatedly.

"Nobody's in trouble." Katie kept her voice even, trying to picture Jeff with the boy. She had no practice at this, but she did know that to get angry was to lose him. "Tell me, what's not real about Christmas?"

She almost said it was her favorite time of the year, but he wouldn't appreciate that. It would be like proselytizing, her knowing he hated it and trying to convince him otherwise.

"There's not a Santa Claus." He tapped again, but

stopped after three times, as if waiting on a response.

"No. Not a real person Santa." Whew. What do you say to that? Katie waited on him, unsure where he was going.

"Konnar's so stupid. That's why I hit him with the snowball. How can he still believe in something that's just a lie?" He looked through the windshield for a moment before looking down.

His eyes were red, and that told Katie something was coming out. Something important. What, she wasn't practiced enough to figure out, but it was there. And important to the boy.

"Karlton and Keithie. Do they believe?"

"Yeah, but they're just kids. Who can blame 'em? They want it to be true." He hit the palm of his hand against the side of his face, sliding it, and it left a damp smear along his cheek.

"You know better, though." She saw a quick nod of his head. "What about the Jesus part? How do you feel about that?"

"They lied about Santa." He brushed at his face again, then balled his fist in his lap. "Why not that?"

"They?" Katie was pretty sure she knew, though.

"Everybody. Even Jeff." He spit out the man's name, as if that hurt worse than all the rest.

Oh, Kevie, Katie thought. "So, are you going to tell Karlton and Keithie? About Santa?"

"No." He frowned at her. "Why would I do that?"

"You did whack Konnar with a rock." She shrugged. "I thought maybe you planned to break the news to everyone."

"Shows what you know. Konnar's nine. He's not a baby, anymore."

"Then, what's the plan this year?" Okay, Katie. What would Jeff do? What was that old acronym? W. W. J. D. What Would Jesus Do? Here it was What Would Jeff Do? She'd seen him in action with the boys. Now she got to leap into the fray.

"Plan?" He said it with a snort.

"Sure. Christmas. You don't believe, because it's all a lie. Your brothers do, and you're not going to tell them. In that case, what's the plan? Are you skipping it all together this year?" This was what Jeff did, called their bluff. She wondered if it would work.

"I can't do that." Not a real answer, just a pronouncement, as if it was an obvious fact, and she should be able to see it.

"Sure you can. You're eleven. You know they don't have Christmas in the Maldives." Thank you, Winnie! "Everyone goes to work. They don't do the holidays or Christmas vacation. No presents. Nothing."

"They're stupid. Everybody wants presents."

"They don't. No Jesus, no Santa. None of it." She shrugged. "Tell your brothers you're going to the Maldives for Christmas, and people would laugh at you there if you had Christmas."

"I can't go wherever that is. That's the stupidest thing I've ever heard." He didn't sound angry anymore, and when he glanced at her, he smiled a bit before he forced it off his face.

"I've got a friend who was going to the Maldives.

They were going to pay her a lot of money if she would go there and skip Christmas, but she said she liked spending Christmas with me, and she turned them down." When he looked at her, Katie nodded at him. "She's coming here for two weeks."

"Does she believe in Santa?" He looked impressed that someone would turn down money just to have Christmas.

"Maybe. I don't know. She acts like she does." And being Winnie, maybe she really did. "When she's around, I pretend like I believe, just for her, because it makes her happy. I think maybe that's why she didn't go to the Maldives."

"Oh." He took a deep breath, like he'd figured out something.

"Does that mean you've got a plan? You know, for Christmas?"

"I might be eleven, but I'm not stupid. We can go, now."

"Okay, as long as you have a plan." Katie started the engine of the Jeep, and shifting it into gear, she released the clutch, and eased it back onto the road. She tried not to smile as she asked, "Is it a secret plan, or is it safe to tell me?"

"I have to have Christmas." It came out heavy, like he was rolling his eyes with his words.

"Like me and my friend. You pretend, and they have a good time. That's a good start. Now, what are you going to do first? Buy them presents?"

"You have to have money to buy presents." He wasn't tapping the window, and that was progress.

"How about decorating a tree? I have one that needs decorating. You could invite all your friends, and it could be like a pretend Christmas party. I'd bring the treats." She smiled at him. Maybe this would work after all.

"Like what treats?" He actually sounded interested.

"Cupcakes?" She shrugged. "Pizza, maybe. Your choice. You choose."

"You'd really do that?"

"Sure. It's Christmas."

"Cool. I want pizza."

"Done deal." She held her hand out, and when he saw it, he grinned and shook.

Two points, Katie crowed inside. One Peavey won over, at least to decorate one tree. She might get something checked off her Christmas list after all.

Ready or not, Christmas, here we come!

8

"Winnie! I'm glad you called." Katie held her phone to her ear with her shoulder, as she ran a stitch of wire through the plastic hook on one of her giant Christmas ornaments. She had one hand gloveless, the better to answer her phone, and her fingers were growing stiff. "We're outside, and it's cold today. If you hear the wind, that's what it is. Still, if I drop my phone, it might sound even worse."

She laughed, but holding a cell phone this way was difficult, that and attempting to manage seven preteen boys decorating the tree by the town gazebo. At least one—Brookie George—was tall enough to reach the top of the tree without a ladder, and that was fortunate, because Katie hadn't thought to bring one.

"We're outside? Sweetie, if you're with Jeffie, of course you're outside." Winnie laughed, and it sounded like she was talking to someone in the background for a moment. “Oh, sorry. That was Ramon. He’s waiting our table today.”

“Ramon, at No. 9? Honey, you better hop out the door. You know you can’t afford anything there.” No. 9 Park was one of Katie’s and Winnie’s favorites, specializing in French and Italian dishes, but it wasn’t cheap. They often chose one option, tasting and sharing, more for the fun of the experience than a filling meal. That was the way of high-end dining, though. Lots of little bites to fill you up, rather than one big dish to load up.

“Oh, no. We’re covered. Hold a second.” Winnie’s voice was muffled, but she was clearly discussing something about the menu. “That was Nikki. She’s insisting Francois join us for lunch. He’s out in the car, and we had to send Ramon for him.”

“They haven’t griped at you, yet?” That wasn’t Katie’s real question, although it was a real question. At No. 9, chatting away on a phone during lunch wasn’t the best of manners. However, her real question involved Winnie being at No. 9, and Katie being here with three half-emptied pizza boxes on the tailgate of Jeff’s Jeep. It didn’t seem fair.

“Nobody knows I’m talking to you, except Nikki, and she doesn’t care. I have one of those ear things on, and my hair covers it. I’m having salmon, with pine nuts, I think. Nikki’s paying.” She whispered her last two words, and she giggled. “So, what are you and Jeffie doing out today? Fishing?”

“We are not fishing.” Katie huffed. “What makes

you think I'm with Jeff, anyway? He's on his boat."

"Oh, we, and you're outside. Oh, oh! I said yes in French, and I didn't mean to. How funny!" The phone scratched for a second, and Winnie said, "Hold on, Sweetie. Don't hang up."

Katie had finished wiring her ornament, plus two more, and at one of the boys' complaints—Jeremy? She thought so, Jeremy Boggs, possibly, if she had the last name matched up—she was restringing longer wire through one she'd done at the very beginning. It had fallen twice, and it needed to be firmly fixed to a branch. Rockhaven storms! It would have to survive at least one, she'd been warned. Thanks, she'd thought. I presumed that's what Thanksgiving was all about.

Redoing the ornament, she heard the sounds of her friend back in Boston making room for the chauffeur slash housekeeper that her second cousin had brought with her from France. It seemed a new place setting had to be sorted out, with apologies, and a quickly spoken string of French flew between her cousin and the driver.

"Sorry. Whew, but that's settled. I know a little French, but when they talk fast, I'm lost. Bon appetite! I know that one. And oui! That's what I said a moment ago, but just by accident."

"Honey, you enjoy your lunch. I've got seven boys here, and this tree will be a mess if I don't give them some pointers." Katie took an ornament from the tall boy, Brookie, and she traded it with a different color, showing him she wanted it on top.

"Seven boys! You do work fast. See you in a

week?"

From over the phone, it sounded like their drinks were being served, but Christmas wasn't for three weeks. Katie started to clarify that, and about then, she dropped the ball she was holding, and it began to roll away from her.

"I'll call you later. Eat something for me."

"Sure, Sweetie. Bye, bye!" Winnie could be heard oohing over something being set on the table as she hung up.

Katie slipped her phone into a pocket; and pulling her missing glove from her back pocket, she slipped it on, calling, "Kern, Matt, reds don't go together. You have to keep the colors separated."

The first one, Kern Pearsons, thin and angular in his oversized coat, giggled, and he poked the second one with his elbow.

The boy Katie had called Matt pointed to a dark-skinned boy across the park who had given up on the tree and was clumping what loose snow he could find under the bushes and tossing it at yet another boy. It wasn't holding together in flight, but rather disintegrating into a miniature blizzard on the way. Only about every third one remained clumped together enough to reach its target. "That's Matt. I'm Paulo."

Ahh. Paulo was light-skinned and blue-eyed. Blond, too, if she remembered correctly. She guessed Rivera as a last name didn't mean much when it came to ethnic appearance.

"Then, Paulo, bring me a blue ball from the box. I've got wire right here." She didn't, but she would by the time he returned.

Snow hit her in the back of her neck, and when Katie ducked her head forward, she felt some of it slip down inside her jacket. She grabbed the chunk of snow that was left and pulled it off her neck, and held it in her hand. She turned to see Matt looking at her wide-eyed.

"Matt. Leaf, isn't it?" He was the dark-eyed boy she'd thought must be Paulo Rivera. "Who was that for?"

"Kevie." That's all he said, but his eyes jumped to the side for a moment, and then back to her face.

"Kevie?" Katie turned to see him just behind her. "That was meant for you?"

"Yes." He stood wide-eyed, unlike the boy who would have run to kick someone a week before. He looked in her hand and back to her face.

"This snowball was meant for you, but wound up down my neck?"

"Um, I'm sorry?" The other boys had stopped to watch, and he looked to them, only finding Katie's face again when she didn't say anything else. "Um, I'm really sorry?"

"You're going to think sorry." She pointed a finger at him, making sure to keep her face stern. Marching forward, she grabbed him around the neck with one arm, just like she'd seen Jeff do, and before he could react, she stuffed the snow down the back of his jacket, making sure to shake the fabric so it would go all the way down.

"Hey," he cried, grabbing at the neck of his coat.

“Are you sorry, yet?” Katie had given up on the stern act, and she was laughing. “Boys, more snow!”

“No!” Kevie cried. “You guys better not!”

“You guys had better! I bought the pizza, and it’s me taking you home.” Katie yelled to them, holding to Kevie with both arms. “Hurry!”

She got as much snow down her coat as Kevie did, because the rest of the pretend Christmas party did just as she asked, except there were too many hands to get all the snow down Kevie’s coat. They were eleven, or within a year either way, after all, and boys that age don’t have a clear and present off switch. That snow had to go somewhere, and any collar was game.

Katie was on the ground, and the snow was going everywhere when a horn honked, getting her attention. She looked up to see Al’s truck alongside the curb. Al called out, waving his hand.

“Never saw a tree decorated like that, before. Wish I was eleven again.” He grinned. “Kevie under there somewhere?”

“Hey, boys, let me get up.” Katie pushed one of the youngsters off, and she stood, pulling her hair back from her face and waving. “On the bottom.”

“Good for you. Keep him there.” Al laughed.

It was Jeff’s voice that made her realize that Kevie’s father wasn’t alone.

“You want to decorate our tree at home later?”

“You did, already.” She laughed at him, brushing his question away with a wave of her hand. “On the dock, remember?”

“I can undecorate it, if you’ll do that with me.” He

could be seen in the truck, nodding his head towards the boys.

"Katie, can I trade Jeff for Kevie? I can take Tim, too, if he's done enough damage." That was Tim Swisher, and he lived out near the Peaveys, but that was understood, and Al didn't say it.

"Sure. I've got extra pizza. You want some?" When he motioned for her to bring it on, she left the boys—the commotion was wearing down, with all the snow used up—and headed to Jeff's car. She sorted through the boxes to give him at least one slice of each kind, and she emptied one of the boxes to load it up for Al. Then she called, "Kevie, your dad wants this," and she held it out for him to take.

"Sure." He ran to her, and he grabbed the box, only pausing when she didn't let go.

"So, how's our plan working? Think your brothers will be fooled?" She noticed Jeff walk up, and he seemed puzzled at her question. She ignored him and kept her attention on the boy.

"Not fooled." He grinned. "Convinced. Bye!" He took the box and was gone.

"Did I hear a little deception going on there?" Jeff leaned and kissed her, putting his arms around her and drawing her in. "What's the plan?"

"Oh, something between me and Kevie." She snuggled in, enjoying the sea-smell of his coat, the smell that told of Rockhaven and boats and winter in a land that wasn't Boston. And she had envied Winnie. Winnie wasn't here. Winnie didn't have Jeff.

"So, how's the plan working?" He murmured to

her, repeating her words to the boy.

"Is the tree decorated?"

"Mostly." He chuckled. "That's your plan?"

"Does it look like Christmas?"

"Pretty much the way I want Christmas to look. No Katie bows, but that's okay. It's the town's tree. Something's missing, though."

"Oh!" Katie pulled away from Jeff. "I let Kevie get away, and we didn't put up the tinsel. He put wires all down it, too."

Sure enough, it was in a pile on the floor of the gazebo.

"Okay. Get these boys to do it."

"It's time for them to go home. Oh, Jeff. What will I do?" She fell against him again. "It was all going so perfectly, too."

"I could do it. You know, a little Santa magic. How would that be?"

"Oh, Jeff!" Katie threw her arms around him, giving him a broad smile. "That's perfect! Santa magic! But it's got to be a secret. You can't tell anyone you did it."

"It's Santa magic. Santa magic is always secret. Otherwise, it's not Santa, is it?"

"Jeff, you are so perfect. Do you know that?" She turned to look at the boys, now tossing sticks at each other. "I couldn't have Christmas without you."

"Without who?" He fought a grin as he said it, and he kept his eyes on the boys as they played.

"You heard me. Without you." She pushed on his chest with two fingers.

"Ho, ho, ho. Without who?" He was fully grinning, and clearly digging for a specific response.

"Oh, you. Without Santa. I get it."

"You do, huh? I'll tell you, Dame Carver, I really am Santa, every year, for all the little kiddos. That means if I string the tinsel, you can really say Santa did it, and every word will be the truth. How does that fit into yours and Kevie's little plan?"

"Perfect, Mr. Claus. Absolutely perfect." She reached to give him a kiss.

"Thank you, Mrs. Claus. Now, you need to get that sleigh started, and get all the little children home. You can start a list on your phone, too, so Santa can know who all the good boys are. Tell 'em you're planning on texting it directly to the North Pole, because you know Santa really, really well. Now, go." He released her and turned, "Boys! In the car, now! Be good. It's almost Christmas!"

Katie thought she would explode with love! No. 9 had nothing on Rockhaven. Nothing at all.

9

"Jingle bells, coconut shells." Katie sang the nonsense words softly as she hummed the familiar tune under her breath. Jeff was in the other room playing with the fire, rather, building a fire in the fireplace, and she could hear the torn paper, the logs clunking, and the occasional snort of irritation when something didn't go exactly right.

"Bryan's coming, you said?" Jeff called to her. Nickerson, he meant, but Bryan could only mean Bryan, one of the "eager beavers" from the snowstorm.

"And Jerry," she called back.

"Little J and Debsy, too?" He yelped, and something fell. "I'm all right," he called out.

"That's good to hear." Katie was in the kitchen wrapping presents, and she'd told Jeff to keep on the other side of the wall. What she was putting under the tree was none of his business.

Her list, not actually that long, was mostly marked off, but the big one was the same unresolved present as before. Ritchey. How was she going to give Ritchey to Jeff for a Christmas present? She laughed to herself, picturing her husband's friend as a jack-in-the-box, wrapped tightly, and springing out at the turn of a handle.

"Jeff, what toys did you play with as a kid?" She was doodling, and it was turning into a box. Above it she drew in an oval with eyes and a nose. "Jeff?"

At no answer, she flipped her pad over—just in case he wandered in—and stepped to the living room. There was the start of a fire, but no real flames. Some singed paper curled off to the side, and one smaller fag of scorched wood had fallen onto the hearth, still smoking.

"Jeff?" Katie pulled on an oversized, fire-resistant glove from atop the woodpile, and stacked the partially burned log back on top of Jeff's carefully constructed stack inside the firebox. Tossing the glove back, she began looking, first leaning into the bedroom to call out, "Jeff? The rapture hasn't come, has it? I expected to go up, too."

She caught sight of him outside hefting a cloth carrier heavy with wood. Seeing the back door partially open, she pulled it wider to allow her husband to step through.

"Thanks, my love." He leaned to kiss her on the cheek as he passed. "Thought I better do this before the fire gets too big."

"Too big?" She nodded that direction with a smile. It was doing nothing at all, except smoking a bit from a fragment of paper that was about to go out.

"I just had it going." His words told his dismay. "Where's Roker when I need him? Do we have more newspaper? I used what I could find."

"That reminds me. I added Roker for tonight, also. Jess, too. When she heard Roker might be here, she practically pleaded."

"I told you that pumpkin pie wasn't just for us."

"The Thanksgiving pie?" A small picture snapped into place for Katie. Roker with his snowshoes walking to their house, and Jess watching outside to catch him just at that exact time. How much bother had it been to bundle up and chase Roker down? Not anyone would have done that.

"Roker loves Jess' pies." Jeff transferred the wood from his carrier to the pile as he spoke. "Newspaper?"

"In the kitchen," she said absently, "but you don't go in. I'll get it, and you never said anything about that pie being for Roker."

"Sorry." He shrugged. "Thought you knew. It's sort of like an open secret, waiting for Roker to figure it out."

"Does that mean there's romance in the air?" She smiled, liking the sound of that. Christmas was for romance, lovers and all that. It was hers and Jeff's first, and she knew it would be special for them. She wanted it to be special for Roker and Jess, too.

"In Jess' air, but Roker's slow on the take. The newspaper? I can go get it myself, if you'd like." He knelt at the hearth, holding a lighter wand in his hand, and his eyes twinkled as he said it. "I'm good at keeping my eyes closed."

"No, you don't, nosy. Still." She wandered in the kitchen and returned with the day's paper. They hadn't read it, but it wouldn't tell anything new, not about Rockhaven, anyway. It was the Globe, and it was all about Boston. Jeff had subscribed, for her, he'd said. She handed it to him. "I think I'll do assigned seats tonight."

"Katie." He held the paper, now rolled in his hand, and looked at her, shaking his head. "It's just a party. Nachos and dip. Assigned seats?"

"Sure. You and me in that chair, everyone else on the sofa, and Roker and Jess in the kitchen." She smiled brightly. "That can be their privacy spot."

"I'm ignoring that. Al and Janine? Heard from them?" He was wadding paper and stuffing it in between logs, but his question said more than just his words. The four boys were normally relegated to the kitchen in cold weather, and the temps were expected to plummet after dark. It was December, and dark meant about four, so it would get cold.

"They can drop off Karlton to play with the Watson-Stryker kids, if he can stay till morning. The rest want to go to movie night."

The Schutmaats had a large garage, and once a month this time of year they moved their cars out and set up a makeshift theater. Children, if their parents accompanied them, were encouraged to attend. It was B-Y-O-Popcorn, but the kids looked forward to it every month.

An unintentional conflict had come up between the movie night and Katie's party. The movie had been scheduled for the Saturday after Thanksgiving, but with the storm, it had been bumped forward to tonight.

The Schutmaats were showing a Godzilla movie, and the Peavey boys had been ecstatic. Al and Janine had given in, apologizing to Katie they couldn't make the evening, but Katie didn't mind. She didn't have the boys' presents wrapped, yet, and she could put it off another day or two.

The phone began to ring. Katie picked it up to see Winnie's number displayed, and she raised her eyebrows, looking at Jeff. "It's Winnie, on the land line."

"Not on your cell." He chuckled and pumped the lighter, and flame shot out. "That's a first."

Katie clicked the talk button. "Hey, Honey! How's your Saturday?" As she spoke, a car door slammed outside. She covered the phone. "Jeff, we have company."

"I'll check." He set the lighter aside and stood. The fire was still dark.

"Sorry, Honey. We have company at the door."

"I know, and I'll be better once you move your car." Winnie bubbled over the line. "Don't you keep your cell on, anymore?"

"My cell? Of course—" Then it dawned on her, it had been low the night before, and she hadn't plugged it in. Here on the island it searched for signal constantly, and that ate her battery life.

"Katie?" Jeff called from the front entry.

"Yes, Jeff?"

"You'd better come see." His words were insistent.

"Hold on, Honey. Jeff needs me. Oh, first, what do you mean once I move my car? It's in my drive."

"I know, and it's in my way. Okay, Sweetie, in our way. Cousin Nikki insisted I come with her."

"Katie?" That was Jeff again, with a certain manic quality in his voice. "We have company, and they're early."

Winnie was here? She'd told her two weeks, but she hadn't thought it would be the two weeks before Christmas. She'd meant the two weeks after Christmas, when she could have her friend all to herself.

Nikki, though? Cousin Nikki from France, via Katie's Boston apartment? She tried to remember if she'd invited her yet, and she couldn't recall actually doing so. Surely she wasn't here, too!

Then the front door opened, and Katie heard Winnie's voice.

"Jeffie! You're so beautiful. Let me give you a hug. Now, enough of you. Where's my Katie?"

Katie was still processing, but when she saw her friend through the beveled glass doors, she felt the smile on her face. She couldn't help it, and when Winnie bounded into the living room, Katie called out, "Winnie, Winnie, Winnie!"

She got exactly the answer she expected when her friend called back to her: "Katie, Katie, Katie!"

It was a huggy kind of moment, even if Katie was still a bit confused. When they quit dancing in each other's arms, Katie looked Winnie in the face, and she asked, "You said Nikki's here?"

"Oui, ma chère. May I sit? It is a very long walk from the car. Francois?" Nicolette held a gloved hand out, and she nodded her head in thanks when he took it to help her across the floor.

Oh, my, Katie thought, her mind racing. She had to come up with three beds, and Nikki could not sleep upstairs. Hers and Jeff's bedroom was the only one on the ground floor, and she had been fighting a slight case of the flu. She couldn't give up her bathroom.

And Nikki? She was used to the best. How would Katie ever satisfy that, and here on Rockhaven, and two weeks before Christmas?

"Winnie," she said, very softly. "I need to move my car?" That was the best Katie could do just then.

"Sweetie, the limo just wouldn't go around. Since it's rented, Francois couldn't risk any scratches. Now, tell me everything that's going on in your life. But before you do, hold that thought. Where's Jeffie?"

"I think . . ." Actually, she didn't know, until she heard her car starting. "I think he's moving my car."

"Good. I need a fire, and I see one right there, ready to go. It's cold up here. Did you know that? I'm glad I brought my long johns." She giggled and said to Nikki, "Cousin Nikki, how do you say long johns in French?"

"Um, caleçon long, perhaps." Nikki shrugged.

"See? Caleçon. I'm learning French." Winnie grinned.

"Non, my dear. Not caleçon. Caleçon long. One is the, how do we say, boxer shorts, and the other is the, um, warm leggings."

"Oops," Winnie giggled again. "My mistake."

"I'm so glad to see you." Katie grabbed her friend's hand in hers, and she squeezed it. She'd forgotten how much she enjoyed Winnie's lightheartedness and enthusiasm for life. She needed this. It would help her get through all the plans she had yet to finalize for Christmas.

"Me, too, Katie, Katie, Katie." Winnie shivered her shoulders, and her hair bobbed up and down.

"Winnie, Winnie, Winnie!" Katie shook her shoulders in turn.

"Ah, d'être jeune. To be young. How lucky you are, my dears." That was from Cousin Nikki.

She had a smile on her face when she said it, and Katie was glad they'd both come. Releasing Winnie, Katie stepped to her cousin to give her a kiss. Although not a real one, the greeting was just as heartfelt. "Welcome, Cousin Nikki. I'm so glad to see you again."

Nikki returned her kiss and shooed her away with the fingers of one hand. She had a smile on her face as she did.

"Is there anything I can get for you?"

"Non. I see Francois returns from the car. He will be my right-hand man." She smiled and waved him her direction. He stepped to Nicolette and stood her collapsed walker at the arm of her chair before he began laying out several medications.

Katie turned back to Winnie, and she grabbed her arms, and they jumped up and down in excitement.

This was going to be a better Christmas than she'd ever thought possible. All the problems in the way? They'd work out.

They always did.

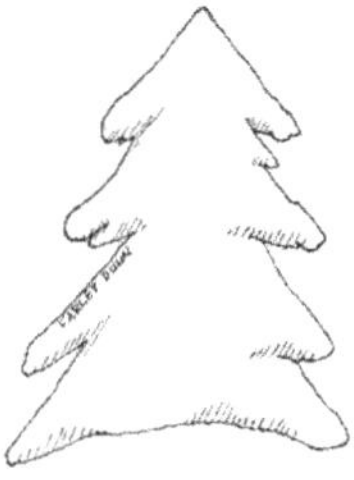

10

"I have a Christmas surprise for you." Winnie teased with Katie, and her eyes twinkled with fun. "You'll never guess what it is."

"And you cannot go in the kitchen." For Katie, Christmas gifts were for Christmas, not for two weeks out. She changed the subject, instead. "How are things at Trinity? Cristina and Alf? Has the baby grown much? I miss Noah. He taught such profound biblical lessons."

"You don't want to guess?" Winnie looked aghast. "Nikki? I come all the way here, and my very best friend doesn't care. What did you say that was? Gross?"

"Grossier, ma chère." Nicolette laughed, repeating the French term fluidly and beautifully. "Gross is your American word for a very large number. You do not wish to say little Katie is a many-numbered person, but a rude person, if you so intend." Her pronunciation of the English version came out more like grass.

"Gross will do fine, because it means something else, too. But since you won't guess, I won't tell you, and you'll have to find out when Christmas gets here. Besides, it's for Jeffie, not you." Winnie didn't look all that offended, rather like it was a game, and she was pleased to still own her secret.

"Sure. We'll let Jeff guess later. Luggage. What about that?" Katie looked brightly from Winnie to her cousin. She remembered the luggage from Boston when Nicolette had shown up in her massively long limousine, and she dreaded how much there might be on this trip. Winnie didn't exactly pack light, and this was the winter season. Cold-weather clothes took a lot of room.

"We brought lots of special stuff. We filled the car. Guess with what?" Winnie cocked her head sideways, with her expression bright.

"A case of broomsticks, and you're late. Halloween was two months ago." Katie grinned, pleased to get in a dig.

"Ahh! I do believe you just called me a witch." Winnie waved one hand at Nicolette. "Katie's being a frump-frump, so she can wait to hear about all the stuff we brought. Now, Noah. Poor, poor Noah." Winnie shook her head and tutted.

"What about him?" Katie poked Winnie on the leg. "That's not fair to say that and not tell me the rest."

"He's in England." Winnie nodded her head at

Nikki. “Queen and country, and whatever else goes with that. Isn’t that right, Nikki?”

“Okay. Explain.” This was apparently something Katie was unaware of.

“You have to remember that Angolan mission trip he took.”

“Did I hear Angola?” The door closed behind Jeff, as he stepped into the room and dropped the car keys on a side table. “Has someone been there?” Without waiting for an answer, he disappeared into the kitchen.

“Noah, one of the lay teachers at Trinity,” Katie called to him. “Don’t you dare look at those presents. I haven’t wrapped them all yet.”

“Your church in Boston. I remember him. Tall, soccer type. Isn’t he on the church team?” Jeff reappeared with two cups of coffee, handing one to Francois, and grinning at Katie. “And no, I didn’t peek.”

“Yes, that’s him.” Winnie let out a dreamy sigh with her eyes closed.

“He went to Angola?” Jeff seemed very interested, and he walked over to sit on the arm next to Katie. “Was it on that trip two, no, three years ago, where that ship was boarded by pirates?”

“You know about that?” Katie was impressed.

“The Anglican Church does keep in touch with its American counterparts.” Jeff chuckled. “I was supposed to be on that trip, but your Noah beat me out for the honors, and now he’s being received by the Queen.”

“No.” Noah Bainbridge? Trinity’s Noah Bainbridge? “I knew they ran into some pirates, but what’s with the Queen?"

"Oh," Winnie said, with a toss of her head, and a flip of her hand, "just a grandson who happened to be on board, there as a representation of the Church of England," and she reached to poke on Katie's arm, "and he was practically saved by our Noah."

"Oh." Katie had no idea.

"That means you can touch someone who has connections with royalty." Winnie held her hand out for Katie to touch.

Katie slapped it, instead. Not too hard, but it was a slap.

"Ow! What was that for?" Winnie kissed the offended spot.

"You're about as close to royalty as I am." Katie laughed. "Get over yourself."

Jeff was looking out the windows at the water, and he fought a smile.

"Ma chère, Katie, do not be too quick to be amused." Nikki held up one finger. "Many Frenchmen make claims to a royal connection, even if our royalty is long gone. Louis XIV had many children, all of which he, um, made legitimate. You have one of these, possibly, in your blood."

"Katie!" Winnie squealed. "You're a royal."

"Not exactly." Katie stood and moved to the fireplace, shaking her head. "French royalty all got their heads cut off, remember? It's called the French Revolution."

"In that case, you can't be my princess?" Jeff teased her. "I always thought of you as my little princess, and now you deny it."

Katie snorted. "Tell me about Cristina's baby. Does it really look just like Alf?"

That brought a chuckle. The truth was that Winnie was coming off a very busy schedule, and she'd only been to Trinity three times in the past two months, and other than her visits to Rockhaven Town Church at the time of the wedding, nowhere else. She'd heard of Noah through Nicolette, who'd become close friends with Mrs. Annie Rosenbaum, Katie's neighbor from her apartment in Boston. Everyone else Katie asked about? Winnie's stash of information was sketchy.

Winnie did drop a hint to Jeff that he had a surprise waiting, but Katie diverted her before she said too much, pointing out the Katie tree out on the dock.

"How pretty! Those are really big bows. Did you put that up?" Winnie patted Katie's knee, smiling brightly.

Katie told her the story, inciting a bit of clapping from her friend by the time she finished, but it was the sleeping arrangements that were on her mind, even with the stories and teasing. Nicolette was the one who cleared that up.

"Ma chère, Katie," Nicolette inserted into a lull. "Francois and I must go before much time is escaped from the clock. Francois can remove your friend's bags, if you wish her to stay. I will have very much room at my bien locatif, if you do not have so much bedrooms."

"Your—" Katie paused to pull her thoughts together, not very quickly, she had to admit. "You have a place? On the island?"

"Oui, ma chère. I should be clear. Bien locatif, um, perhaps, property rental. I would not ride the big boat back and forth unless very necessary, non? There is, Francois? Round Road, you say?"

"Non, mademoiselle." He continued in a short speech of fluid and very beautifully spoken French.

"Oui, oui. Merci." She smiled at Katie, tapping her temple with her fingertips. "It is Round the Island Road. How should I forget? Eagle's Roost. You may know of it."

Katie shrugged, but Jeff chuckled. "What?" Katie asked him.

"The big place? The shingled gateposts?" He spread his hands to indicate how wide each one was.

"The De Groot house?" Katie had been there once. It was out towards her family's property on Carver Point. She'd wondered what the De Groot heirs had done with it since the grandparents were gone.

Jeff shook his head. "Bigger. Three miles this side."

"Oh." Katie pictured the home he was talking about. It wasn't ocean front, although she was certain the acreage across the road that fronted the shore was part of the property. The appeal about Eagle's Roost was its location on one of the highest points on the island. From Lookout Ledge near Carver Point, the Eagle's Roost could be seen rising from the trees. It was the island's most exclusive estate, behind gates triggered by electric eyes and powered by private generators.

It offered unparalleled 360 degree views, and had been featured in numerous architectural magazines over the years. No one Katie knew had ever been inside. Now she wondered just why her cousin had bothered with her little apartment. It must have seemed a shoebox compared to her home in France.

"Sweetie, do you have room for me?" Winnie smiled brightly. "I just need a little space, and a bathroom, of course. No outpotties."

"Outhouses," Katie automatically corrected. "Are you sure? Cousin Nikki's place . . . I suspect you would love Eagle's Nest."

"Oh, Sweetie, I came to stay with you. Fancy houses don't make Christmas. Best friends do." She held out her arms for a hug.

"That is so sweet." Katie grabbed her and hugged her back.

"Inside bath?" Winnie whispered it in her ear.

"Inside bath." Katie found that funny. She remembered last July and the seal that blocked their path to the outhouse. Winnie had been a trooper, and they'd had a great time. Now, though, she required a bathroom. Duh! It was freezing outside. This time Katie couldn't blame her.

"Good. Then I'm staying here." Winnie ran a hand down Katie's smooth hair, and she let out a very satisfied sigh. "Now, presents. We brought presents. Jeffie, Francois, follow me."

"We've already got a Santa." Katie called to her. "Jeff."

"That's what I said. Jeffie, Francois, come be Santa. We came loaded down."

Jeff looked at Katie and rolled his eyes, shaking his head. Katie shrugged, and with a laugh, she shooed him after her strawberry-blonde friend.

Cousin Nikki sat tapping her finger against the arm of the chair. She hadn't said much during the biggest part of the conversation, and that was when Katie noticed the earbuds in her ears. A music player lay on the arm of the chair, and Nikki was gazing out at the scenery, tapping in time to her private musical fantasy.

Nikki, Katie thought. My only real family, come all the way to Rockhaven just to see me. How much better could this get? She had her new husband, her best friend, and her only blood-relative here for Christmas.

Now if she could just get Ritchey sorted out for Jeff. Ritchey, get yourself up here. Katie didn't know if she could do it, though. In the past week, he'd become a very difficult man to attach a message to.

He wasn't replying to a single one.

11

Jess arrived first, of course with a pumpkin pie in tow. By then Jeff had the fire roaring, and Winnie and Katie had bags of chips opened and ready to dump into several big bowls. The afternoon's family gifts and all those from Nikki's car had been delegated to an upstairs bedroom, and a very special decoration had been added over the kitchen table. A twig of mistletoe was tied to the kitchen light.

"This is beautiful," Winnie exclaimed over the pie.

"We call it Roker pie." Katie reached over and took it from her and moved it to the side cabinet.

"Roker . . . isn't that Jeffie's friend? Did he make it?"

Katie saw the red around Jess' neck, and she pulled her into a quick hug. "Love you, Jess, and your pie, too. Thanksgiving? He ate a quarter of it just putting it in the kitchen. I got three bites."

"I should have made two." Jess was very soft-spoken, and she studied her hands. "Will Roker be here soon?"

"Roker, you, are you two a couple?" Winnie smiled, pointing to Jess and to the pie.

"Stop it, Winnie." Katie pushed her hand down. "Roker doesn't know."

"Oh. You want to be a couple. I know some guys like that, too. They don't know I exist."

"Oh, they know." Katie laughed, as she pulled the dip from the fridge. "They just know better."

"Oh, you can be so mean. Come on, Jess. You and me, let's go where we're wanted, like in any other room. Katie can join us when she gets her polite on." Winnie said it all with a smile, and she waved over her shoulder as she dragged Jess away.

At a knock on the front door, Katie heard Jeff inviting Roker in, with the big man's buoyant voice carrying throughout the entire house. He called to Winnie and Jess, telling them he was heading in the kitchen. Katie overheard Winnie telling him he was not, and that made her smile. He was going to sit down in front of the fire and keep an eye on it with Jess.

With small plates and napkins on the counter, and bottles of water and soda lined neatly up, Katie stood back and admired her preparations for the Christmas party. It looked pretty festive, if she did have to say so herself, and the invitees were arriving right on time.

"Chips," she said to no one in particular. Pulling out the chip bowls, she turned two bags over, filling them, and stood back, pleased. She crumpled the packages into a sack off to the side and set it on the floor. The only thing left was to heat the cheese. She set it in the microwave and started the timer.

Earlier she'd taken time to welcome Bryan and Jerry, and of course Jerry's kids. She had heard others coming in, since, and had accepted deliveries of baked goods for their after-nachos snacks, but only Nina Vinson had stayed in the kitchen to help.

"I live in a kitchen, and I'd be lost in there without a spoon in my hands." Nina laughed. "Besides, I'm not frying, and that's nice."

Nina had brought makings for home-cooked eggnog, and she stirred away at the stove. Two gallons of milk and a carton of eggs were in the pot. The empties were off to the side, and she tapped her spoon on the rim and slipped it in the sink.

She had dropped in a bowl of spices, telling Katie that it was her grandmother's recipe, and she'd promised never to divulge the secret mixture. Katie would enjoy it, though. Customers at Harbor View did every year.

Nina had brought something else. Off to the side nestled a bowl of powered cocoa. Add it to the eggnog, and it was hot chocolate to die for. The rest would go in the ice bath in the plastic cooler Nina had brought. Hot cocoa, but chilled eggnog. It would be perfect either way.

Katie's stomach growled. She looked forward to it.

"Hungry guests." Jeff leaned in, his shorthand reference coming with a wink and a grin. "If we don't want them to start gnawing the walls, we might need to get the nachos out."

"Have Al and Janine dropped off Karlton, yet?" Katie pulled the melting cheese from the microwave, and she tested it with one chip. "Almost perfect, even without the dip mix. Jeff?"

When she held the bowl out, he took a chip from the table and dug in, smiling in satisfaction. "Thanks. I was going for the front door trim in about a minute." He scratched at the door frame to emphasize his reference to a hungry beaver.

"My restaurant door has a few gnaw marks on it." Nina patted Katie's arm with a knowing smile. "Can't feed a man too fast or too often. Get that dip mixed in, and he won't be able to resist."

The front door slammed, rattling the glass. It opened again, the second time closing much more gently. Something fell over in the living room, and the talking got louder.

"Katie?" Janine appeared in the doorway. "Hi, Jeff, Nina. Are you sure Karlie's okay with you all night? We can stop by after the movie, but it'll be late. Al said several families are going, and Tom might do a double." A double feature, she meant, but her listeners got that.

"You have a good time. He's fine." Katie put her bowl down and took Janine's hand. "Jeff's a good enforcer. We've got extra lobster traps out back if we can't control him. You brought clothes for church?"

"By the front door, and thank you. You're the best. Karlie's been a pill tonight, and I was afraid he'd disturb the movie if we had to drag him along. You guys have fun with the party." She grabbed a chip with a laugh, and dipping into the cheese, she put it into her mouth as she headed out. She could be heard greeting several people in the other room, and wishing them a fun evening.

"How long until I send in the crowd?" Jeff returned, and at his side was a five-year-old pounding on his waist with clenched fists. He pulled him up, and held down his arms, asking him, "Hey, and that's for?"

"They won't let me play in the fire." The boy's face was screwed up as if he was about to cry.

"And quite right. I won't either." He smiled as the boy wrapped his arms around Jeff and laid his head on his shoulder, sniffling. "Katie?"

"Five minutes. I need to mix the dip in the cheese. Just five, okay?" She held up her opened hand, showing her outstretched fingers.

"Five. Then here they come." He winked again, and leaving, he leaned into the boy's ear, "And how long was your nap this afternoon?"

"I didn't have one."

"Oh. Maybe that's part of the problem . . ." His voice disappeared into the general hubbub in the other room.

"He's going to make a good father, that one is." Nina had poured the bigger portion of the eggnog into metal ice cream canisters buried in the ice filling her plastic chest. She placed the plastic lids on and covered them with more ice. Then she dumped coarse salt over them. "There. I don't make ice cream, but I make good use of my ice cream tubs, anyway. Now, hot chocolate, and we're good to go."

Cups of steaming cocoa, complete with sticks of cinnamon, soon spread across the unused half of the counter. Katie called for Jeff, and he made the formal announcement that it was time to eat. After a short prayer, those gathered at the Ragsdale household for an evening of fellowship and good times began to fill the kitchen.

"Where's Karlton?" Katie stood with Jeff in front of the fire, and she had his arm wrapped with hers. The diners were drifting back in to find anyplace they could to sit and enjoy their food. A couple had made it to the deck, but it was long since dark, and she didn't expect they would remain long.

Later, there was a gift exchange planned, but it was meant to be comical, and there was no real rush. The wrapped boxes and gift bags were on a table in the foyer, festive and bright, but now was for food.

"Out. He was gone before I could get him to the bedroom. I put him on our bed for now."

"Ahh." That made Katie smile. "We'll leave him until everyone's gone."

"My thoughts exactly." Jeff chuckled.

When the hubbub settled to the crunching of food and subtle conversation, Winnie stepped beside Katie, holding a steaming cup of cocoa. "Have you tried this? It's good. Like chocolate eggnog."

"It is chocolate eggnog. I'm ready to go for my food."

"Don't you dare!" Winnie held out one finger,

pointing firmly. "Privacy, first!"

"Privacy?" That was Jeff. "It's a kitchen, and the door's open."

"No, Jeffie, it's mistletoe land." Winnie scrunched her shoulders and giggled. She pulled out her phone and clicked it on.

"You didn't!" Katie grabbed the phone. She tapped the camera icon and pulled up the latest picture. There were Roker and Jess, in Jeff and Katie's kitchen, their arms wrapped around one another, almost directly under the mistletoe.

"Roker?" Jeff pulled the phone from Katie's hand. "And Jess?" A smile spread across his face.

"If that's the way it is, I need something." Katie took Winnie's cup from her, and she took a long draught of cocoa. When she was finished, she smiled appreciatively. "That's good."

"Told ya'. Winnie knows best. And, you're welcome." Winnie smiled, but she took the cup back, anyway.

Love was truly in the air, and that was the best news in the world for Katie. She wanted everyone to share in how much she loved Jeff, of course with their own partners, but to share, anyway. If Winnie had a hand in that for Roker and Jess, then she'd accept it. Winnie did know best, and she was glad she'd come to the island two weeks early. It had been the perfect thing to do.

"Can we try it out next?" Jeff leaned down to kiss Katie on the nose.

"Try out what?" Katie frowned.

“Silly.” Winnie poked her on the shoulder. “The mistletoe, of course.”

“The mistletoe, of course,” Jeff repeated, kissing her this time on the cheek.

“Just do it.” The gruff words were from Kent, Nina’s husband.

And Jeff did, and Katie knew one thing for sure. She couldn’t be happier if she had all the money in the world. And since she didn’t, that was okay. She had Jeff, and he held her in his arms, and that was the most anyone could ask for.

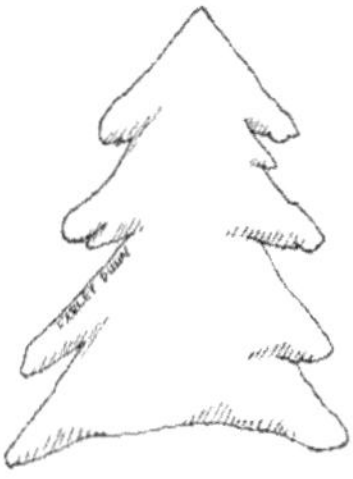

12

"Don't forget." Katie tiptoed just a fraction, to give her husband a quick kiss on the lips. "Al and Janine need us this afternoon."

"The ferry ride?" They were outside the church door, greeting arriving parishioners, and he glanced at the late-morning sun and squinted. "Least the weather's pretty."

The ferry ride was about Janine's father. He'd died several months earlier, and he'd wanted his ashes poured into the sea. Off the ferry into the sea, to be exact, and returning from the mainland, not the other direction. Jeff and Katie were on the support team.

"I think everyone's here. I'm heading inside." Katie released Jeff's hand and pulled her hair back from her face. "It's chilly today." She missed Winnie being at services on this special Sunday, but her

Cousin Nicolette was having a slow morning, and they were having "church on the hill." Katie had told her to look for her email after service. There would be a quiz that evening.

"Did you see the tree?" Jeff took her elbow before she could get away and nodded the direction of the Town Park. They could see the gazebo from the church steps, and the decorated tree was just to the side. It was now wrapped in glittering tinsel. "I think Santa's been busy."

"Oh, Mr. Claus. Has Kevie noticed it?" Katie hadn't seen it, and she was thrilled. It was beautiful, filled with the magic of Christmas. It was proof the holiday spirit even applied to eleven-year-olds.

"I think so. Perfect timing, especially if we're doing the ferry thing today. Anyway, it's cold, and you need to get indoors." He kissed her on the cheek and nudged her inside.

During the service, Katie gave up her normal seat at the front of the church, and she joined Janine and the kids. Al was with the communion team, and he was sitting in a special section closer to the front of the building. Karlton was next to Katie, with crayons and a Jesus coloring sheet. He worked on the back of a hardcover hymnal, intent on his own private version of crayon perfection. The other boys were the other side of Janine, not perfectly behaved, as they were scribbling notes or passing pictures to one another, but they weren't disrupting the service, either.

The message was about Joseph, and the forgiveness he gave his brothers, even after they sold him into slavery. Jeff tied it into Jesus, who would one day come in a manger, to be sold into slavery. In the children's story, Jeff had told of Moses, and how he was kept safe in a straw basket, and how that was almost like a manger, and invited the children to bring their parents to view the live nativity scene the following weekend beside the gazebo. Did they know Roker? Of course they did, and several of them turned to point to him on the communion bench. He would be Joseph. Come see him in a white beard.

Jeff's story reminded Katie of the previous summer, and how angry she'd been at God for taking her life from her, and how, when she'd opened back up to God, he'd given it all back. Jeff had been here on the island waiting, even when Katie had railed against God for stealing him away. She hoped she could make the connection with Janine that afternoon that what God takes away with one hand comes back to us in the other.

After service, Jeff and Katie joined their friends at the Peavey's home for Sunday lunch.

"It's just cold shepherd's pie." Janine set the casserole dish on the table along with a serving spoon. "With this afternoon, I—I've been too frazzled to think about any real cooking."

"The movie last night is partly to blame. Godzilla II ran past midnight. No cooking happened after that." Al grinned, and he took Janine's hand, looking in her eyes. "We love shepherd's pie, honey, cold or hot. Sit and eat. There's nothing else you need to do."

Katie knew all about the Godzilla movies. Three of

the boys had ridden out with them, and the two youngest had brought Godzilla figurines, reenacting the movies, line-by-misremembered line, on the way over.

Katie stood behind her chair. She had done the drinks, ice and tea, and milk for the two youngest boys, even taking it on herself to refuse to serve soda to Kevie and Konnar. Then, Al had popped a soda to pour into a glass of ice, and Konnar's face had darkened. It wasn't Katie's house, however, and she had shrugged it off.

Kevie, though, glanced at his father and back to Katie, trying to fight a grin. He seemed to find it funny. Maybe he was growing up after all.

Leaving the church, Kevie had made sure to point out the tree and the tinsel as they drove by, asking Katie who had done that. The ornaments? She made sure her question sounded perfectly innocent. It was somebody special, she was certain. No, Kevie had demanded. The tinsel, he'd whispered to her.

Katie had replied that she'd last seen the tinsel inside the gazebo. It had been Kevie's job. Hadn't he? Once his dad had come by, she'd left to take the rest of the boys home. Jeff? she'd asked. You?

Wasn't my tree, Jeff had replied. Must be magic. Santa magic.

Kevie hadn't looked entirely convinced, but he hadn't called them on it, either. In Katie's book? She was certain he wanted to believe, and if he couldn't, he wanted his brothers to.

She was certain she heard him whisper to Keithie, his youngest sibling, that Santa had decorated the tree.

"Katie?" Jeff reached to her chair and scooted it out a bit, jarring her back to the moment. "Ready?"

"May I give the prayer?" Katie took in Al's quick glance at Janine, and Janine's face filled with gratitude.

"Thank you, Katie." Al nodded. "Boys, bow for the minister's wife."

"Minister's wife." That was Kevie, and he snickered the words in a whisper. "It's Katie, Dad."

"Shush." Janine reached and poked him on the arm. "Bow your head and show respect."

"Anytime, Dame." Jeff had a grin on his face as he cut his eyes her direction.

"Heavenly Father, these are my friends, and they make up my life. Kevie, Konnar, Karlton, Keithie, and Al and Janine. What would I do without them—"

"What would we do without you and Jeff?" That was Al's mumbled comment.

"Anyway, God, today is special, and we ask you to be there for us, for everyone, and let us feel your love. And Lord, thank you for the food and the hands that prepared it. Amen."

"Hands off, Konnar. I'm first." Kevie grabbed the serving spoon out of his brother's hand.

"I guess they're hungry." Katie looked at Jeff and chuckled. "That tells me cold shepherd's pie must be very good."

"Janine's is the best. However, do I fall into the friend category, or somewhere else? I didn't hear my name in there." He had a laugh in his voice as he spoke.

"Don't know. Where do you want to be?" Katie caught Janine's eyes, and she was attempting to keep from laughing.

"Ouch," Jeff said, as he dished up a spoonful of pie. "Should I have asked?"

"Silly." Katie nudged him with her arm. "You're the minister. How's that verse go? The two shall become one?"

"You can't win, Jeff. Give it up." Al said that.

Katie laughed. Al was right. She had already won, over two months before, when she and Jeff had held hands and said I do.

Katie shifted the conversation a new direction, quietly asking Janine, "Are you taking your car on the ferry this afternoon?"

"Ferry? We taking a ferry ride?" Keithie, four, overheard that just fine. His face brightened with excitement.

"Dad," Kevie began. "It's Avengers on TV. It starts at four."

The two middle boys had their Godzilla figurines out on the edges of the table, and they were having a mock battle.

"Janine, you told them, right?" Al looked at her questioningly.

"Oh, Katie, Jeff!" Janine's eyes filled up, and she fled the table.

"I guess she didn't. Sorry, you guys. Enjoy lunch." Al stood and went after her.

"Oops," Katie said. She had no idea she would set off the waterworks. It had been months, after all.

“Okay, Konnar. More pie?” Jeff stood and held the spoon. It was an undisguised distraction.

“Pie?” His plastic figurine stopped, and he looked up, finally interested. “What kind?”

Some days are better than others, thought Katie. This one? It looked like it was going downhill quickly. Still, the sun was shining, there was good food on the table, and Al and Janine had their best friends to prop them up.

She just hoped they had their sea legs on. She suspected the ferry ride back from the mainland would be an hour and a quarter of messy waterworks.

“Kevie?” Katie waved her hand to get his attention. He was pouting. When his eyes turned to her, she said, “Four, you said? If we get away from here early, we can set our machine to record it. How’s that?”

“Can we?” His eyes found the clock on the wall. “What time—” he snuffled “—do we have to leave?”

Katie looked at Jeff. “Your guess?”

“Ten minutes. Take the Jeep.” He shrugged. “Have fun.”

“You are a hoot, if I ever saw one. You should give me more warning next time.” She nudged him again with her elbow, and she wasn’t easy about it.

“I do what I can.” He smiled. He was spooning more pie onto Karlton’s plate.

“Kevie . . .” Katie turned to the boy, to see him already shoveling food into his mouth.

“I guess that means you need to get busy. Eat, woman.” Jeff kissed her on the cheek before digging into his own plate of pie.

Katie dug in, too. It was over three hours plus the stop by the house. She'd be hungry by the time she returned. What was she thinking? Who cared about three hours in the future? She was hungry now.

She shoveled a bite in, and she began to chew.

13

Katie and Jeff stood alongside the ferry railing overlooking the sea. Jeff's Jeep was beside them, with Al's truck just behind, the only two vehicles making the trip. They were on their way back to the island, and in spite of the bright sun, it was cold, being December and all. Janine and her bunch were inside out of the wind.

Jeff wore a loose coat, and Katie was snuggled inside with him as best she could. His arms cut much of the wind, but her face was cold.

"Look!" She nodded alongside the boat to a gray form swimming just below the surface.

"Your seal," Jeff said softly. "That means you're home."

"You softie. Earlier, that was very touching, the kids each dropping in ashes." Katie still had the picture in her mind, and she supposed she always would. Janine had a plastic bag partially filled, and one at a time she'd poured a small amount into each boy's hand and let him fling it off the side of the boat. Then, together, she and Al had emptied the bag. Janine had pulled Al tight and whispered, "Go, Dad, the oceans are yours forever."

"Thank you for supporting them. Al and the kids have been important to me. Janine, our friend from all those years ago. We have to stick together." He had his head next to hers, and he rubbed her hair with his cheek.

"Or we have nothing." She murmured the words.

They were passing between Settler's and Rockhaven, and the tide was high. All the rock ledges were covered, and the sea had eaten the shoreline to the base of the trees. Then, Settler's Island disappeared behind the ferry, and more and smaller islands filtered by. Soon, they would pass the headland leading into Rockhaven Harbor, and they would be home.

As the town came into view, Katie looked for the church steeple. It had always been special. Now? It was hers.

"Look, Jeff, a cookout." Sure enough, a thin column of gray smoke twisted skyward not far from the church.

"I see." There was something else in his voice, though.

"What? Are cookouts not allowed?" She wanted to laugh at him, except that he wasn't laughing with her. "People do have cookouts on Sundays."

"That's from the park."

"The park?" There were no facilities for outdoor cooking at the park, just the gazebo, the tree the boys had helped her decorate, several granite benches, and a grassy expanse of lawn, now winter brown. "Who would be—"

"Hang on, Katie." Jeff had his phone out, and he put it to his ear. "Al, get up here. I think we have a fire in town." He listened a minute and replied, "Near the park. Do you want to call it in, or should I?" Then he said, "We're up front. Come decide for yourself."

"You think it's . . . serious?" Oh, Katie hoped not, not this close to Christmas. How horrible that would be, to lose your house right before the holidays truly got into swing! And there were houses right next to the park.

"It's not black." Jeff took a deep breath, pulling away from her when Al walked up to look at the rising smoke.

Katie understood. Wood burned clean. Fabrics and petroleum-based products didn't. If it was a house, it would burn black.

Al turned from the view, and he had a phone to his ear. One hand was in his hair, and he looked down. Someone must have picked up, because he raised his head and looked back toward town, pointing, as if whoever it was could see.

"Jeff?" She took his arm. "If it is a fire, what then?"

They were arriving at the landing, and Jeff exhaled loudly. "You go with Janine. Al and I'll take the Jeep.

Better get in the truck before we finish docking." He kissed her and pulled out his keys, and he disappeared into the car.

Katie caught that he hadn't really answered her.

"Katie, is it anything?" Janine was just coming out of the passenger area. The boys were running for the truck, calling out claims on various seats.

"I'm riding with you." She shrugged. "Al's going with Jeff."

"Oh, not a fire now." Janine had her hand on the door handle, and she looked across the town. In front of her, the Jeep was already running. "Might as well climb in. We'll know when we know."

Across the water, a siren started up, and they could just catch sight of the town fire truck speeding down Main, with all lights flashing. A couple of trucks flew past after it, with one small and rusted station wagon bringing up the end.

"Al's a volunteer, right?" Volunteer fireman, Katie meant.

"Everyone is out here." Janine started the truck, and as Jeff's brake lights flashed, they watched him tear past the ramp—nearly level with the high tide—and across the empty lot. "Al's lead, though. I don't have a good feeling about this."

"Not the church, I hope. Can we drive by?"

"No choice." They had to drive by the church, unless they circled the entire island, but her words told that. Janine put the truck in gear and followed much more slowly than Jeff had exited.

"Mom," Kevie urged, "faster. I want to see the

fire." He pointed over the seat to a rusted four-wheel-drive speeding by. "There's Chipper. He'll probably get tangled in the fire hose."

"Will not!" That was Konnar, and he yanked his brother back and began pummeling him.

"Boys." Janine shook her head and turned right towards town. The smoke was thicker, and it was lighter in color. "That's good. Look at that, boys. White smoke."

"Ah," came their disappointment from the back seat. "They'll have it out before we get there."

"Why is white good? Thicker smoke means the fire's bigger, doesn't it?"

"Not white. That's steam from the fire hose." Janine downshifted, and they turned the corner towards the Town Park down from the church.

The big red truck was there, with lights still flashing, and three men wore regulation fire-fighting equipment. Jeff, Al, and several other men were around, moving equipment and talking to concerned citizens. Cars lined the streets on both sides of the park, and half the gazebo was blackened.

"Cool!" That sounded like Karlton. "Look at that, Keithie. It almost burned down."

"What did?" It was a little boy's voice, meaning it was Keithie's.

"Goon, look!" That was Kevie. Something smacked, and Keithie yelped in response.

"Boys!" Janine said that sharply, and the noise quieted. "There's your father. Let me go find out what happened. Katie, do you mind waiting?"

Katie motioned her on. She watched Jeff, so much in control of the situation. As if people deferred to him, just because he was Jeff. Being minister might have something to do with that, or maybe people just liked him, and they knew he would step in and help out in whatever situation came about.

Kent from Harbor View crossed the street just in front, and Katie waved back when he lifted one arm to her.

As Jeff walked to the truck, he waved at her with a smile, and she rolled the window down.

"Hey, is it out?" She reached to take his hand, and she smiled when he squeezed it back.

He nodded and leaned into the truck, calling to the kids, "Glad Santa got that garland up. It would have been toast left in the gazebo. Yea, Christmas." He shot the boys a thumbs-up sign.

"Could you tell what happened?" Katie could now see that one of the suited firemen was Roker. He'd removed his helmet, and he was talking with Chipper, she thought.

"Roker thinks electrical. There's an old plug around the back, but I'm thinking early fireworks. Dry leaves and a bottle rocket. It doesn't take much." He grinned. "I remember a few times I nearly started a fire or two."

"Oh, you do, do you?" Then it hit Katie. "That's where we planned the nativity. Jeff, it's next weekend."

"We'll find a place, but it's not as bad as it looks." He pulled her hand up to kiss it. "Only this side's burned. Maybe we could rename the holiday this year, call it Fired Up For Jesus."

"Ooh, kissy, kissy!" Keithie called it from the back seat.

"You'll think kissy, kissy." Jeff released Katie and pulled the back door open. He leaned in and pulled the four-year-old forward and planted very noisy raspberries all over his arms.

"Yuck!" he screamed, but all the boys were trying to push Jeff away, and it was more fun than anything else.

"Boys!" Janine climbed back inside, shaking her head at the scene in the back. "Al's heading to the firehouse to help clean up the truck. Jeff," she called over the seat, "Al said you can pick up Katie at our place. He'll catch a ride with you."

"Sure thing. You, boys, are lucky your mom's driving away. You, Karlton, were next in line." They squealed, and he laughed. "Bye, Katie. See ya'." He leaned over the seat and kissed her on the neck.

As they drove off, Janine thumbed the direction of the boys, and she said, "You know, Jeff can take any of these home anytime he wants. Al and I don't mind at all."

Katie laughed, but she would rather wait for one of their own. If it looked like Jeff, it would be the most beautiful child on the island.

She pressed on her stomach, feeling just a twinge of nausea. That fire, and at the gazebo. She guessed the success of the nativity worried her more than she thought. Oh, well, come Christmas, things would settle down, and she'd feel right as rain.

She felt something wet hit her neck, and pulling it off, she saw that it was a spitball. She turned, and narrowing her eyes, she said, in as stern a voice as she could muster, "Whose is this?"

Three of the boys pointed to Kevie. He shook his head, but he didn't point at anyone else, and with a wicked grin, Katie unsnapped her seatbelt, twisted around, reached over the seat, and grabbed Kevie's knee. Then she squeezed it, laughing when he began to beg for mercy.

When she sat back in her seat, she noticed Janine watching her. "What?"

"The ones Jeff doesn't want, you're welcome to." Janine grinned and turned her attention back to the road.

As much as she wouldn't have thought in July, Katie actually liked the boys. In small doses. Take them? No. To live with them would make them a pain in the neck. She wanted to be able to enjoy them instead.

"Thank you, Janine. They're good kids."

"Not really." Janine looked at her, and she laughed.

"Some of the time, maybe." Katie laughed with her.

"Like when they're asleep."

It was a good day, even with the burning of the gazebo, and Katie looked out the window, enjoying the sun shining on her face through the glass, and thanked God for friends like Al and Janine, and for her wonderful life on Rockhaven Island.

It was everything she'd hoped it would be.

14

Katie was bundled, and it was a good thing. She stood on the town wharf, and the wind whistled past her hood, doing its best to reach chilled fingers inside to nip at her ears.

The week since the fire had been a nightmare of mishaps, and she pushed them aside. Today? They had awakened to a brisk north wind, and the men in the church had decided it was perfect for racing sailing skiffs in the harbor.

Katie's take? They were crazy, and now, because they were crazy, she was frozen. Her nose, anyway. Even the knitted scarf she had around her face didn't cut out every bit of the wind.

"Look at that." Nina nudged Katie's arm. "Kent's been in the water three times, and he's still trying to win. If he gets himself sick, we may have to shut the restaurant down for a week."

"Maybe he should. You could use a vacation." Katie twisted to look at Nina, peering at her from her knitted cave. "Stay inside where it's warm. Now, that's a good vacation."

"You're right, there." Nina laughed. "Where's Winnie? I thought you two were joined at the hip." Before Katie could respond, Nina grabbed her elbow and pointed to the water. "In red, that's Ada. She's beating all the men."

Sure enough, someone in a red waterproof suit sat astride a small craft with a tightly trimmed sail, and it flew across the waves, almost hidden in a blur of scattered spray.

"Ada Simpers?" Katie pulled her scarf down a bit to make sure she was heard. "From the market?"

"The same. She's a competitor, I tell you that. Often wins, too."

"I'm impressed." Katie was, and that was a fact.

"Thought you might be out there. I see Jeff. He couldn't talk you into it?" Nina had an impish look on her face, what could be seen of it.

"Haven't felt well." Katie touched her stomach. "Indigestion or something. It comes and goes." It had, too, and she had begun to suspect it was a long-term type of indigestion, the sort that comes from loving a man too much, and perhaps from not being careful enough.

"Ah," Nina said, in a knowing way. "Kent's and my children are long gone, but I've felt that way before. Have you been to the clinic?"

Katie noticed she didn't call it a hospital, and she smiled at that, but she didn't want suspicions to get out. If it wasn't what she suspected, well, this was a very small community, and she'd be fending off inquiries by the hour. They would all mean well, but she didn't want to go there.

"Shush." Katie put her finger to her lips. "We've got company—" half the town standing on the wharf watching "—and I'm not sure, so . . ." She left the rest unsaid.

"Speaking of company, there's some on the way." Nina pointed to Katie's side. "My lips are sealed. And, we're still on for Monday."

"Thanks, Nina." Katie gave her a quick hug. Monday was the Town Hall Banquet, and it hadn't come together yet for Katie. In fact, not at all. Winnie—globe-traveling fashion model—had poo-pooed her difficulties and said she knew what a good banquet needed. Katie should leave it in her very beautiful and capable hands. Then, somehow, Nina had offered hers and Kent's help, and Katie had felt just unwell enough that she'd had to let it go.

She was glad she did, too. She'd learned a Christmas Sunday children's musical was expected from the minister's wife, and even with parents volunteering to help, she'd struggled to keep ahead of that.

"I'm off to cheer on my husband. I'll be at the nativity tonight. Bye!" Nina waved and wandered off.

"Hey, Kevie." Katie put her gloved hand on his beanie-covered head. "Why are you not out there?" His three brothers were picking up small pieces of gravel and chucking them in the water, totally preoccupied in their own little worlds.

"Tonight. Mom said I might get sick." He shrugged, as if that was an excuse he didn't really mind.

"Tonight. You're still one of my wise men, then." She pulled her scarf down to speak, so he could see her smile.

"Yeah. You know, part of the plan." He shrugged again, but he grinned.

"Sunday, too? Lighting up the Christmas miracle?" She had given him a special job in Sunday's musical. A scary one, but a job she was sure he'd enjoy. It involved fireworks.

"Of course." His face lit up with a smile.

"Is the plan working?" It seemed so to Katie, her part of it, anyway. She had Kevie involved, and that's what she'd intended.

"Think so. Dad said he's never seen us be so good."

"Which one's your dad?" She pointed to the water. The boats were all over the place. Sometimes it seemed less a race than a mad cacophony of exuberant enthusiasm, but they all managed to round the turn markers and generally head in the same direction.

"See the Ninja Turtle? That's mine, and Dad's using it." He pointed, grinning broadly, clearly having fun with his father fighting for the prize underneath a Ninja Turtle banner.

"Oh, that's too good. I'll make sure Jeff never lets him forget it."

Katie looked up to see Nina back, with Jess from up on High Road. Jess carried a cup of steaming cocoa, and Nina had two.

"Thought you might like one." Nina held a cup out. "They've got more, Kevie. See Matt's mom. She's serving with Mrs. Boggs and Mrs. Swisher."

"Cool," he said, calling to his mother in a folding chair down the wharf, "Can I have hot chocolate?" He was running her direction as he said the words.

"Boys," Nina said, shaking her head. "Too much energy. Jess is here to cheer on Roker. I told her she needs to do more than cheer him on."

"Oh?" Katie had the drink in her hand, and she drew in the aroma. She wasn't sure drinking it would sit well, though, and she hesitated. "What should Jess do?" She pulled her scarf down, beginning to regret wearing it, as it wasn't really that warm, not with pulling it down so often, and she took a sip of the cocoa. She enjoyed the heat more than the flavor, and she kept her hands wrapped around it.

"Snag that man. He's been single too long." Nina grinned mischievously. Jess looked down and shook her head, but she smiled, too. "Back to your friend, Winnie. I got distracted by Ada a few minutes ago, and I apologize. Did she make it down today? I'd hate for her to miss the fun."

"There." Katie pointed down the town lot to where the front of Cousin Nikki's limousine could be seen just the other side of Jeff's Jeep. "She's keeping my cousin company. Staying warm, too." Katie grinned, but she was envious.

"Nikki? She's better?"

"Some." Word had been passed the previous weekend that she was having trouble getting around, and while she had Francois, Winnie and several of the townies had been spending time giving her attention and help when needed. Katie had run out with a casserole from Nina and a pie from Jess one afternoon, but with her stomach, she'd barely made it back home. After that, she'd given Winnie the keys to her car, and told her to make good use of it.

"Think sharp, ladies. They're heading in." Nina called it out, and the crowd's attention shifted to the water. Janine was standing, and all four of her boys were at the railing, cheering for their father.

The pending finale trumped all other discussion, and the entire wharf was riveted to the small boats jumping over the ragged whitecaps. Undulating tides of animated support burst forth when the occasional sail dipped into the churned froth.

Jeff was out there, but Katie hadn't tracked him well. He was in light gray, with a blue slash across his chest. It was a borrowed suit, and the boats were similar, generally with white sails and light-colored hulls. In the cacophony of motion, with the continual spray misting the scene, the boats sometimes disappeared from view.

Jeff had been lost to her most of the race.

"Roker!" Jess clapped excitedly. "There he is, in second!" She began to cheer him on to go faster.

"Daddy, Daddy," the youngest two Peaveys yelled, jumping up and down.

As the skiffs passed the finish line to the cheers of their respective supporters, one at a time they made their way to the town float at the end of the ramp. Neither Al nor Kent came in first, and Jeff didn't seem to be in the running. Ada Simpers took third. It was Roland Heyniger that claimed the blue ribbon, and on his arrival, his teenage daughter and two of her friends jumped up and down, hanging on his arms, squealing, and almost pulling him off balance.

What Katie didn't see was what began to worry her.

"Roker?" She pushed through and caught him on the arm. His face was flushed, but he glowed with excitement. Jess had an arm wrapped in his on the other side. "I can't find Jeff."

"Ah, not to worry." He laughed. "Jess and I are headed to pick him up. I was just telling Jess here, he went over at the far turn marker—"

"And he broke his rudder." Jess finished for him. She looked brighter and happier than she had since Katie had been on the island.

"The boat, I'm sure he tied it up at the Zwecker's. It's why I didn't finish first." Roker grinned and shrugged. "But you notice I didn't stay to help. I still wanted to win."

"That's Aidan's house, right?" It was at the end of a built-up jetty. Aidan and his wife Tatiana were summer residents that were at the wedding but gone two weeks later. The Zwecker's float was in, but their wharf would allow Jeff to moor the boat to a piling and make his way up the rock ledge that formed the original foundation for the jetty.

"Want to ride along? We'd haul the boat and bring it back, but in this weather, it'd be best to motor out and tow it in."

Even to Katie that made sense. The wind was whipping the waves into ice cream froth. Much stronger, and the race wouldn't have taken place at all.

It took longer to walk to Roker's truck than to drive to Aidan's. Jeff had hiked the 300 yards from the wharf to the drive beside the house, and he was huddled out of the wind on their porch, waiting. He waved when he saw Roker's truck making its way down the narrow street.

"Hey!" He threw himself into the seat and slammed the door after him. "Katie, nice." He took her hand and held it to his face. His suit was wet, although he would be dry on the inside, or mostly dry, as going in the drink would allow some water to penetrate even the tightest of seams.

"Second!" Roker held up two thumbs over the seat.

"You'd have been first if you hadn't slowed for me." Jeff clapped him on the shoulder. He began to peel his gray outer suit off. "I was okay. You should have gone on."

"He had Katie to think of." That was from Jess, and she glowed, with her eyes twinkling. "What would he say if you drowned, and he hadn't at least slowed down?"

"Aha, good friends, aren't we all? Slow down to watch the minister drown." Jeff grinned at Katie. "See what they think of me?"

"Just a jumpstart to the great sailboat race in the sky, that's all." Roker was turning his truck around, but it had four doors and a very long bed, and the road was very narrow. He'd already backed it up and pulled forward three times, and he called to Katie, "Mailbox, starboard side. Be my lookout."

They made it with Katie's precise instructions, and with Roker's careful driving, they were on their way back to the party. It would be a party, too. Most attendees at the race were gathering at Harbor View for cocoa, if they had other plans and couldn't stay long; and a late lunch, if they were hungry. Regardless, it would be warm inside, and after enduring the wind, warmth was what they needed.

For Katie it was more. She had asked the members of her nativity scene to stick around. They had the final plans to pull together, and a few costume details to stitch up. Also, with the wind, there had to be room under each costume for long johns, coats, and gloves. No one was catching pneumonia on her watch.

In addition, Katie wanted to see how the banquet was pulling together. It had been her baby, with decorations, a tree, and special music. She had planned to shine, bringing Boston glamour to the island year-rounders. With feeling ill, and Winnie "practicing her French" with Nicolette, she had no idea how things were coming along.

There was the limo, though, just down from Harbor View, and Katie was relieved. She missed Nikki, too, and she hoped to catch up with her. Roker let them out at the door.

"Save me a seat," he called with a wave as Katie shut her door.

It was indeed warm inside. Race attendees were sitting around in various-sized groups, four here, one long table with over a dozen, and in the back by the windows were Cousin Nikki, Winnie, and Francois. The chauffeur stood to the side, and at one point, he helped Nicolette adjust her chair.

"Ah, ma chère," Nicolette called out, when she saw Katie and Jeff walking up to the table. She held a hand to Katie and called again, "Ma chère, my little Katie. Come, a kiss."

"It's good to see you, Cousin Nikki. Has Winnie kept you good company in that big house?" Katie gave her the expected "air" kiss and hugged her by gently resting her hands on her shoulders.

"And so many others. I did not remember that I still know people who live here. It has been magnifique. How do you say, magnificent. I am sorry we do not see so much of each other, but, what shall we do? It is the way it is." She motioned Katie closer, and she reached a hand to touch her cheek. "You, I do think, must be very happy. You say unwell a few days past; I say very happy."

Katie was surprised at that. In English, unwell did not mean happy, and at this moment, she was feeling the qeasies quite strongly.

"She is. You know, happy." Jeff put his arm around her, and he chuckled. "Even if I didn't win."

"Last place." Roker was coming in, and he called it loudly. "Jeff didn't finish, and that's worse than last.

She picked a loser." He grinned and pulled up a chair from an unoccupied table, then a second one for Jess.

"Says the loser who left me out there." Jeff laughed to those seated at the table when he said it. "A broken boat, and he sailed right on by."

"My, my!" Winnie's eyes were wide. "I thought you men were good friends. When did that change?"

"Ho, ho," Roker chortled. "Don't you worry about that. Rockhaven men change friends about as often as they change underwear. Jeff's stuck with me as long as he's on the island."

Katie had just pulled her chair up, and she dropped her forehead to the edge of the table. She was laughing so hard she thought she might cry.

"Roker! TMI. Now, look what you've done." Winnie patted Katie on the head. "He doesn't mean it, Sweetie."

Katie raised her head, still laughing, and she wiped her eyes. "No, it's picturing the stuck together part. It adds a whole new meaning to a man not changing his, um, well, you know."

Roker looked mystified. "TMI? What does TMI mean?"

Jess was bright red, and Cousin Nikki? She had her lips pursed, and if anything, Katie would have said she was fighting a smile of her own. However, she couldn't stay to find out, because her stomach did a flip-flop, and she had to run straight for the ladies' room.

"Katie?" Winnie went after her, calling, "Katie? I promise, Roker didn't really mean it."

Katie did make it, if barely, her queasy tummy spoiling what could have been a very nice lunch. At least, there was one good thing. One sip of cocoa wasn't much, so there wasn't much to come up, and for that, she was truly grateful.

15

"Roker, you are the most handsome Joseph I've ever seen." He was, too. Being a bit rough and burly fit perfectly with the shepherd persona he was to portray. Katie thoroughly approved.

"Thank you. I never expected to find myself in a dress, though." He growled the words, shaking his head. "Wearing an Arab hat, too."

Roker had a striped, loose-sleeved costume on over his heavy winter gear, and a contrasting cloth on his head, secured with an elastic rope. He was perfectly in character, and Katie wouldn't listen otherwise.

"Have you seen Jackie?" Jackie Schutmaat was scheduled in for the role of Mary, and Katie hadn't seen her. At lunch earlier, she hadn't given any indication she'd be late. Off to one side, Jeff knelt, adjusting Konnar's shepherd robe. She called to him, "Jeff, have you seen Jackie?"

Before he could answer, someone else called to Katie.

"Me! Me! I'm Jackie for the night." It was Jess, running up in a snowsuit, with mittens on her hands. She carried her costume, one in three blocked colors: an inner robe, an outer one, and a headpiece similar to Roker's. "Tom's under the weather, and Jackie asked me to trade. I had to stop by and pick it up."

"You two get baby Jesus and wrap him up for the manger. Make sure only his face shows. We don't want him to get frostbite." Baby Jesus was a life-sized doll, and it was in a sack next to the gazebo.

"How's it coming?" Jeff came up behind her and put his arms around her. "I see your angel's ready to go. The gazebo's not too bad, is it?"

Winnie was the angel. With her halo hair, she was perfect, as if she did indeed have an angelic aura surrounding her head. Her complaints before Katie convinced her to take the job? Not so angelic.

The gazebo, with its half-burned structure, was unrecognizable. It was now draped with fabric, in undulating swathes, much as a Middle-Eastern tent might look. One section was pulled back, revealing steps leading into the unburned section, and the inside was illuminated. The entire structure glowed.

There was activity all over the park, and the areas where people were working were lighted by gas-powered lanterns or car lights. The Swishers had goats, and three of theirs were staked on the grass. Babbitt George, Brookie's father, owned a horse he rented out in the summer, and it was in a blanket near the curb, hobbled to keep it from wandering off. Babbitt was off moving the trailer out of view, so as not to ruin the effect. Brookie had a curry comb out, and he brushed at the animal's flanks.

Katie heard a generator start up, and numerous floodlights winked on, shining where the individual characters would be standing. She had called on Kevie to help her stake out everyone's position that afternoon, and Al had come up to position the lights. He disappeared into the gazebo and came out with a portable lantern, turning a dial and extinguishing the flame. The tented structure still glowed, so Katie knew a light had been installed in there, also.

She had some concerns about the weather. During the sailboat races, the sky had been clear, with full sun. The wind had brought in clouds that afternoon, and the sky had turned murky. The air was still, but it was bitter. If it rained, they would have to move everything to the Town Hall, and the night was specially planned as a drive-through nativity. No one had to get out of their cars; just drive by and enjoy the experience. The Town Hall was a viable option, but only if they wanted half the attendees.

"Please, God." Katie looked skyward, even though it was dark, and she couldn't see anything. "No rain. Please, no rain."

"And if it does, Tinka's brought a basket of ponchos and umbrellas. We'll be fine." Jeff's voice whispered his assurances in her ear. Tinka was Rod DiLalla's wife. Rod ran a lobster boat—as did Jeff—as well as attended Rockhaven Town Church.

"You eternal optimist." Katie patted one side of his face with her hand.

"The eternal optimist needs to check on the camel. We'll see if it works." He kissed her cheek and moved off towards the horse.

Katie knew the story behind the camel. It was the George's horse. A special saddle had been rigged with a foam topper, and a brightly colored sheet would be its disguise. It wasn't exactly a camel, but as close as they could come on a murky and cold Saturday evening in December Maine.

She actually thought it was funny. The goats? Those were a good substitution. They'd considered a cow to stand in for the ox, but good sense had taken hold, and that was the reason for the goats. Cows tended to leave gifts, and cleanup afterward had to be considered.

Jeff clapped his hands loudly, and he called, "Attention, everyone. It's about to start. Fifteen minutes."

Sure enough, just where Main turned into Round the Island Road, two cars waited behind a sawhorse barricade, their parking lights on and their engines running. The night's presentation already had guests, and everyone wasn't in place.

Katie searched out Winnie. "Honey, is there anything you need before we start?"

"A hot tub?" She smiled, but it was a pleading smile, not a happy one. "It's cold out here."

"You did wear your gloves?" Katie lifted the sleeve of the angel costume to see that her friend did indeed have substantial gloves on her hands. "Long johns? You remembered those?"

"Two pair." Winnie bounced up and down. "Maybe I can warm up like this. Look out. Incoming."

"Keithie!" Katie turned just in time to catch him. The small boy grabbed Katie's leg and hid behind her. "Hey, say hello to our angel. Who do you think this is, Michael or Gabriel?"

"Don't care. Keep Karlie away."

The other brother came running up, and tried to grab at Keithie's arm. Katie held up her hand. "No, he's with me. You know Kevie and Konnar are shepherds, tonight."

"Want a real Jesus." That was Keithie, and it was muffled into Katie's leg.

"But Jesus is here." Katie knelt and tapped on the boy's chest. "We can't take him out of here and put him there. That's why we use the doll, instead."

"Don't care. Want baby Jesus."

"Karl, would you want to sleep in your crib, again?" Katie had a tactic in mind, one that hopefully would answer the smaller boy's concerns as well as alleviate whatever they were fighting over.

"That's stupid. That's for babies." He snorted in disgust.

"So, Keithie, do you think Jesus feels the same? He was a baby, and he grew up. He doesn't want to be a baby again."

"Okay," he mumbled. "You're it." He tore off after his brother, leaving Katie wobbling.

"Winnie?" She held out her hand. "Help me up?"

"Okay, Sweetie. It's time to get me in place. Help me with my ladder?" Winnie smiled. She pointed down the street to where more parking lights glowed, and as they watched, another car pulled up and dowsed its driving lights. "We've got more tourists, and I want my angel to be real."

It was simple to do. The two pulled a stepladder from the gazebo and opened it, setting it up just behind the manger. The baby Jesus was already inside, and his smiling face was their point of reference. When they were sure the baby would be looking at Winnie, they tossed a sequined cloth over the ladder, and spread the extra fabric out over the ground, giving it the effect of a snow-covered mountain.

"Let me help you up." Katie held a hand out to steady her friend.

"Coming down might be the problem." Winnie hiked her white angel robes up to reveal jeans and heavy outdoor boots. "Unless I fall, then you can put me back together again."

"You're not Humpty Dumpty, so quit whining. Just sit still once you're up there, and it'll be fine. Is Nikki coming?" That was to distract Winnie. "She looked tired at lunch."

"I hope so. She's my ride home." Winnie was to the top, and she'd let go of Katie's hand. "Make my skirts pretty."

"If I can take your shoes off. Here, let me pull this down." Katie yanked at the bottom edge of the costume to get it to cover the boots, causing the ladder to wobble in the process.

“Careful.” Winnie slapped her hand away. She reached in a pocket and handed Katie her phone. She smiled brightly. “I need to post a picture. Take a pretty one of me as an angel.”

“Not really possible.” Katie backed up, turning the phone on and pulling up the camera icon. “Does this phone have an angel app?”

“Angel app? Sweetie, just take the picture.”

“No, I’ve seen them. You take a picture of someone, and the app adds a background, like Santa or a scuba diver. You said you wanted an angel picture, and that’s the only way I can think to do it.”

“Oh, you. I am an angel. Already. Now take it and give it back. I want to post this before the train starts.” She put her hands on the top of the seat and smiled prettily.

“Smile.” Katie held the phone up.

“I am. Take it.” Winnie’s words sounded forced.

“Bigger!”

“Katie!”

A hand reached over her shoulder and tapped the icon to take the picture. “Done. Five minutes. I’m moving in the camel now.”

“Thanks, Jeffie. Phone, Katie.” Winnie held out her hand.

As the characters moved into place, the spotlights making them seem more than just townies wearing hokey costumes, Katie was filled with satisfaction. One thing. Just this one thing had finally come together, and if she could get this to work successfully, surely Christmas would happen right on key.

"Hey, how's the tummy?" It was Nina, and she reached to pat Katie's stomach. "Any more incidents?"

"Not since lunch, and thank you for not saying anything." Katie smiled. "This is pretty. The whole town's come together to do this, and just wow!"

"You've pulled us together to do this." Nina took her hand and patted it. "Thank you. Oh, there's Kent, about to move the barricade. Looks like Roland's got the other one. It's showtime."

The spouses and others who had helped set up were gathered across the street from the park. Nina had provided more of her eggnog cocoa, and it steamed in several hands. The remaining lanterns still burning were extinguished, leaving little more than glowing eyes where their mantles still cooled. The only lights were on the nativity characters and baby Jesus, with the glowing, tented gazebo in the background.

"Oh, Nina. I had no idea it would be so beautiful." Katie felt tears come to her eyes. "Do you really think everyone will love it?"

Darting across the road, the two youngest Peaveys ran into the park, yelling, "It's really Christmas. Yea!" Al chased after them, pulling them back across the street, as they yelled, "Hi, Kevie! Look at you, Konnar!"

"Somebody does. Before I forget, I picked up something for you at the market. Here." Nina pulled a fist-sized box from her coat pocket, and she slipped it in one of Katie's pockets. She patted Katie's stomach again. "Just so you know for sure. I'm headed off to stand by Kent. Congratulations for this. It's all due to you, and don't think we don't appreciate it."

Katie watched her walk away. She had intended to grill her on what was happening with the Town Hall Banquet, but it had gotten away, and now she was gone. Somehow, she didn't trust Winnie to pull this off.

She pulled out the box enough to recognize what it was before slipping it back inside. She closed her eyes and shook her head. This was what she didn't want to happen. Still, Nina had been very discreet, and as she said, this way she would know for sure.

Jeff walked to her as the first cars began to pull by, their parking lights on and their headlights off. He wrapped one arm around her. "You did it."

"Not by myself." She pulled his arm tighter. "Look," she pointed. "I think it's snowing." Small flakes were starting to fall, and already, several cars had wipers undulating across their windshields.

"For you. That's God's way of saying Merry Christmas."

"It is, is it?" She smiled, wondering what made him say that. It was sweet of him, no matter.

It was only minutes before the wind began to pick up, and the snow increased by a power of ten. The dead grass was soon crusted with white, and the fabric on the gazebo flapped with enthusiasm. The participants in the nativity were holding their robes around them, and the goats bleated incessantly. Katie thought the sound effects, if anything, were on the money, but the snow? Maybe it had snowed in long-ago Bethlehem. If so, this was the most accurate nativity she'd ever seen.

They actually held it together for forty-five minutes. Anyway, by that time, there were no more cars, and the road had disappeared under the snow. Katie fought the wind as she helped Winnie to the ground, only to have the ladder blow down and tumble against the gazebo as soon as it was vacated.

Securing all the nativity equipment was a nightmare, and by the time they had things in place, Katie was almost in tears.

Not even the nativity had gone right, and it had started out perfectly. Would Christmas fall apart, too? What else could go wrong?

Even Winnie ran off and left her, headed back to the big house on the hill with her Cousin Nikki.

It was riding home with Jeff when she went to put her gloves in her pocket and remembered the box from Nina. She was glad it was dark, because all it did was make her want to cry.

Pregnant, and at Christmas? How would she get everything done?

16

Sunday morning, and the wind whistled off the water. Snow still whipped the landscape just outside the window. Katie hadn't felt like eating, and she was cold even with the oil heater running full tilt.

"Jeff, you're sure we'll have services in this?" She turned to him, both wanting to stay inside and watch the storm from the protection of her window-filled room, and knowing the importance of the children's program that was the entire morning service.

"No one's called in and bailed. Islanders are a tough bunch." He leaned in from the bedroom, his shirt undone, and two layers of long johns showing underneath. "Besides, it's supposed to clear. Weatherman's promised."

"You are a Mainer through and through." She smiled. She supposed her words could be interpreted to mean his pragmatic attitude, but she had noticed the long johns.

"Oh, what gives you that idea?" His words came through with a laugh.

"You know how to stay warm." Even so, she was bundled up in about as many clothes. Her legs would be exposed during the service, but she had heavy leg socks with open feet ready to pull over them for the ride to church.

She should give in to pants and insulated outer-wear, but she hadn't bridged that gap, yet. Sunday mornings were for fine clothes, dressing up in the best one owned, and showing God's glory to the world. At least that had been her world in Boston. Services at Trinity had sparkled with diamonds, gold chains, and designer boutique finds across the auditorium.

Today was all about mufflers and scarves, and trying to stay warm.

"I like it when it does this." Jeff stepped up behind her, wrapping her in his arms, and kissing her on the temple. The wintry scene beyond the warmth of the glass looked out across Moffat Cove, and past the dock extending into the water. The tree filled with Katie bows shivered in the wind. Jeff's boat moored farther out rocked, pulling against its mooring, fighting the thick, gray water. It was barely visible in the sideways-driven snow. "As long as I don't have to take my boat out."

"Tonight? Will you cancel?" She didn't have to explain her question. Out in the boat, she meant. Jeff would get that, as this was the biggest, most important boating event of the year. For Jeff, at least, even if no one else was out.

"Hardly." He kissed her again, before withdrawing to continue dressing for the morning services.

Katie sighed. She wanted tonight to happen, and she wanted to go along, as Mrs. Claus. It was Jeff's yearly Santa tour. He put a lighted tree on the boat, filled it with candy and gifts donated and wrapped by diligent church members, and motored around the island to all the docks that were lighted and had waiting carolers singing. He pulled the small gifts from the tree to hand to the carolers.

Last year he'd finished after midnight, Ada Simpers had warned. She had a summer cabin on Otter's Reach, and she'd been one of the last. She hoped he got to her earlier this year.

Her phone rang, and she stepped to her purse to pull it out. "Katie, here."

"Hi, Sweetie. It's snowing! How exciting! I can see the whole island from here."

"I can see my tree from here. So, you like the snow. Stay through February, and I'm told you'll get all you want for a lifetime." Katie smiled. She pictured Winnie jumping up and down with excitement, and it lifted her spirits.

"Are the kiddies still doing their thing at church? You see, I kinda promised Nikki, and she's been in there all morning with Francois choosing her most Christmassy ensemble." She whispered, "I suggested a Rudolph sweater we found under the stairs, but I don't thinks Nikki's into sweaters."

"I wouldn't think so. As far as the musical, Jeff says yes. We're about to leave. Do you have my quiz questions from last Sunday?"

"I didn't think you were serious." Winnie giggled. "Besides, I've been doing Christmas stuff, so who's worried about an old quiz? Oh, there's Nikki." She sounded like she covered the phone and called out, "That's beautiful. Everyone loves candy canes." She whispered back to Katie, "Rudolph would be more fun, but I think she's wearing a Sorbier. I've always wanted to model a Sorbier. Nikki's so lucky."

"Rich is the word. What's Sorbier?" It sounded like an ice cream drink.

"Oh, you poor girl. You really need to come on a fashion shoot with me. He's French haute couture with a capital H. Oh, look, Francois has on real clothes. I think he's coming, too. Isn't that exciting? Nikki says she used to attend services at your church, and she wants to check out your honey. That's Jeffie, if you didn't know. What do you want to do this afternoon?"

"Who's that?" Jeff stepped from the bedroom, pulling a tie around his neck. With the morning's musical, he was excused from his ecumenical robes this week, and it was his chance to show he did own a tie. Normally, it was casual wear under the robes.

"Winnie." Katie covered the mouthpiece. "She won't slow down. I did get one thing from her. Do we have plans this afternoon? She wants to do something."

"I have to deliver my gifts. I am Santa, after all." He grinned, adding, "Mrs. Claus."

"What time do you start?" She uncovered the phone. "Hold a minute, Honey. We're discussing this. We're working around Jeff's Christmas plans."

"Three-ish, but I have to have time to get dressed and the boat loaded. That means I should be back here by half past one. Lunch, then?" Jeff was pushing the knot of his tie to his neck. He nodded the direction of the phone, indicating Winnie. "Ask her if she wants to be an elf."

He laughed at that.

"Do you speak elf?" Katie grinned, speaking into the phone. "Santa and Mrs. Claus need a helper to deliver presents."

"Another Christmas party? How exciting! Where's it at?"

"On Jeff's boat, and on every dock that has carolers out waiting."

"Oh." Winnie sounded disappointed. "We don't have a dock, or a boat. I don't guess we can come." Cousin Nicolette didn't have a dock or boat was what Winnie meant.

"No, you ride on Jeff's boat, and we deliver presents to other people's docks. It'll be fun!" Katie made sure not to mention the blowing snow and overcast skies. While the snow was beautiful outside, and it might give them a white Christmas, without the sun, the wind would carry a bite. She tried to sound bright and encouraging. "You could hand out the gifts."

"You could have it here. There's plenty of room." Winnie's lack of enthusiasm for being a Christmas elf on a Maine lobster boat was apparent.

“Okay, Honey. Wimp out, if you want. But you’ll be at church to see the musical?” Katie got the message.

“Time, Katie.” Jeff interrupted as he pointed to his watch, and he draped his overcoat across one arm.

“We have to go. Be there. Promise?” Katie moved away from the window, snatching her thick leg socks from the chair on her way to the door.

“Both of us. Miss you, Sweetie. I’m so excited about lunch!” And she clicked off the phone.

“Where are we going?” Jeff lifted Katie’s long coat and held it for her to put on.

“Oh! I didn’t ask.” Katie looked at her purse, and the phone she’d just dropped inside. “I could call her back . . .”

“We only have about three choices, anyway.” Jeff smiled, twisting his shoulders in a shrug.

“Harbor View, I know.” Katie laughed. “The others?”

By then, she had her coat on, and she turned to Jeff and rested her forearms on his shoulders, looking into his face. He was so handsome, and in his suit, who’d ever picture him out on a lobster boat, trolling for traps, and hauling lobsters from the depths of the ocean?

“Here.” He pulled her to him, and he kissed the end of her nose. “However, if we’re coming back here, no one else is invited.” He kissed her nose again. “I want you all to myself.”

“I already promised.” She enjoyed his attentions, though. “Besides, I don’t have anything prepared.”

“If we’re here, you don’t need anything prepared. We won’t have time to eat, anyway.”

“Oh, you!” She slapped one shoulder. “What else do men think about? We’d better head out, lover boy, if we want to be on time. If we don’t go now, we’ll be late for meet-and-greet.”

“They’ll understand.” He kissed her this time on the corner of her mouth.

“Not.” She did kiss him back, though, and she didn’t miss.

17

"Debsy, you hold this, and when Joseph says, It's a boy, you wave it high in the air."

Katie was presenting the children's musical *The Bethlehem Star*, and Debsy was the star. Rather, she would be holding the star. She was dressed in a silvery angel costume, with a tinsel halo, and all she had to do was walk behind the manger and hold her glittered foam star on a stick.

However, the girl just didn't seem to understand what Katie wanted her to do.

The rest of the cast was on the other side of the makeshift curtains stretched across the front of the church, already acting out their performance before the church members. Katie and Debsy were still hidden from view, and the musical was winding down. Katie could hear the events she couldn't see. Little J and the two youngest Peaveys formed the rest of the star brigade already standing around the manger, but Debsy was the piece de résistance. Her star was five times the size of the others, and it would lead the shepherds and the wise men to the baby Jesus.

Debsy had to get this right.

"I need to potty, Miss Katie." Debsy put her hands over herself and began to jump up and down. She called it out rather loudly, and scattered laughter could be heard from the audience on the other side of the curtain. Most of them had seen at least one rehearsal, and they had a pretty good idea of what was coming next, as well as who was playing the part. Debsy didn't have a quiet voice, or a subtle presentation, not at three.

"Now?" Katie held the child's face and whispered her question. "It's your time to go on."

"I can't hold it. I can't wait." She continued to dance.

Katie glanced up to see Kaylene Watson-Striker, Debsy's mother, peering around the end of the curtain.

"Miss Katie, I'll take her." She motioned to the girl with her hand, and Debsy took off running, her silver angel costume billowing around her legs.

Now Katie was in a pickle. The music was building again, and it was to the part where the lights would fade, and the sparkler team—incidentally made up of her tree-decorating boys, led by Kevie—would run in waving sparklers over the manger to simulate the miraculous power of God come to earth, and not so incidentally, to disguise the moment of the birth of Christ.

It was a kids' musical, after all. Then, Debsy's part was to march to the back of the manger, raising her star for everyone to see. Without it, the wise men wouldn't know to start their march.

The lights dimmed, and Katie cringed. This was the critical part of the morning, the one thing she'd included that would be a blinding success, or her total downfall. The sparklers had been her idea, and she had no idea how they would play out. It was Kevie, after all, leading the festivities.

The room brightened, flickering, and at the laughter of the crowd, Katie knew the fireworks were on the way. She waited for Debsy, wondering if she would be brave enough to make it backstage in the onslaught of darkness. Probably not, Katie surmised, preparing to stand in for her part. That's what a director was for, and the kids wouldn't think it too odd. She'd filled in as the Star of the East in most of the rehearsals.

The fireworks burned themselves out, and as the lights came back on, Katie stepped through the curtain holding her star high. There was scattered applause, and one, "Where's Debsy?" from the auditorium, but the shepherds, two of them carrying stuffed animals, and the third dragging his by a plastic leash, came up one side of the church. On the opposite aisle, the Wise Men trudged along in ten-year-old pomp and glory.

As the final members of the cast gathered around the manger, Katie felt a tug on her dress. She looked down to see Debsy holding her hands up for her glitter star. Off to the side, Kaylene waved with a smile and headed back to her seat. Gratefully, Katie passed on the star, and moved the curtain aside to disappear backstage.

She was relieved when the announcer read, "And the Bethlehem Star leads the faithful, even today, unto Christ." The lights went down, and applause started, with one or two call-outs from the crowd.

Katie was glad it was over.

When the lights came up, she worked her way back through the curtain to announce that as soon as the cast members were out of their costumes, they were free to go, and to thank all the parents for coming out in such blustery weather.

"I think I liked the first angel better." Jeff stepped to her, still in his suit.

"You did?" Katie knew just what he meant, and she smiled. There would be no enduring kisses offered or taken in church, but his smile told his feelings.

"Go," Jeff told her. "Bryan's promised to help for a few minutes, and we'll look after this. Your friend's in the back chatting up Roker. Go save him." He grinned, pointing. Sure enough, Winnie and her strawberry halo obscured part of Roker's face.

"He's a big boy. Is Jess helping out at the restaurant?" If she was, that's where they were going, and they were making sure Roker was with them. After Winnie's matchmaking at their house, those two weren't going to be allowed to go their separate ways.

Bryan stepped up with a canvas bag, and he held it out to Jeff and Katie, sort of like a peace offering. "Can we start? The wife wants to get home to lunch before long."

"Katie, we'll be just a minute. I'm sorry." Jeff leaned in and gave her a quick kiss, and he turned back to the stage and began working the curtains to the side.

Katie wasn't sorry. She had worked with the church women to put it all together. She was happy to have someone else pull it apart. Kern, one of her sparkler boys, was sitting on the third row, probably waiting on his mother, and he had a small ball he bounced continually on the floor.

"Kern, how'd the sparklers go? I was behind the, um—" She pointed behind her, to the men taking the curtains down. "—and I didn't have a very good view."

His face lit up. "It was cool, Miss Katie. Nobody's ever let us have fireworks in the church before. Paulo and Kevie and Jeremy and me want to do a Fourth of July show, too."

"You do?" Katie laughed. She bet they would. "I'm glad you had fun. You boys have been the best, with the tree, and everything. Are you planning on caroling for Santa tonight?"

Not everyone on the island lived on the water, and Kern was one who didn't. His parents lived on a hill up on Second, with a greenhouse they maintained year round. However, just like everyone on the island, people who didn't live on the water invariably knew someone who did.

Those who didn't, or more likely, who were on the outs with those who did, could show up at the town float on Main. That was available to everyone, no matter how well they got along with their neighbors, and if they were singing, it would be one of Jeff's stops.

"Brookie's dad said me and him could stay the night with Kevie." He grinned as if that were a big deal. "Mom said thank goodness."

"Kern?" His mother called from the back. Unlike her slender son, she was stout, a true Mainer. From Down East, she liked to brag, as if the hardiest Mainers came from there.

Katie supposed they did. She understood the weather was more brutal there than here, but it seemed to Katie she was still a Flatlander, and those in the interior could better lay claim to be called the toughest residents in the state. Still, Kern jumped when she called, waving to Katie, and with a "Bye," he was gone.

It was Nicolette in the foyer who seemed to be the Grand Dame of the morning.

"Merveilleux, my little Katie." Nikki held her hands out for a kiss from her only niece.

"You are so kind, Nikki." Katie reached to her and gave her the perfunctory pseudo kiss. She touched the very puffy sleeve of her dress in admiration. It was flamboyant in a crisp and festive red and white. Katie understood the candy cane reference from earlier. "You are beautiful this morning. I understand this is a Sorbier. Do you know the designer?"

"Oui." Nikki smiled, looking very pleased. "C'est un très bon ami."

"Help me out, Cousin." Katie laughed. "I didn't catch that."

"I know!" Winnie had her hand up, and she came

running to join in the conversation. Her interjection caused Nicolette to smile.

"Sure, Honey. You can barely say bon appétit. No cheating, either." Katie looked to her cousin, to see her with her hand held just in front of her lips.

"She said he's a good friend. See? I am smart." Winnie beamed.

"Nikki?" Katie couldn't believe this.

"Oui, ma chère. Franck and I, we have known the other for a very long time." Nikki waved one hand dismissively, as if it were a matter of no real interest.

When Katie and Winnie got to themselves, Katie pulled on her sleeve and demanded an explanation. "You, Honey, do not know French. How did you know what Nikki said?"

"And you, Sweetie, do not know designers. How did you know that was a Sorbier?" She tossed her head flippantly, and she had a superior smirk on her face.

"Um, I asked . . . you."

"Sorry. I'd forgotten. Besides, what do you think Nikki and I talked about all the way to the church? Clothes, Sweetie. I wear them, and she buys them, all the best designs. So, there. Who's smart, now?"

Katie had a pretty good idea. She had open-footed knitted socks for her legs, and Winnie sported bare ankles. Winnie might shout fashion, but Katie wouldn't get frostbite.

Before she could point that out, Jeff and Bryan appeared from the auditorium, Bryan carrying the bag, now stuffed with the curtains, and Jeff holding the wooden manger, now folded flat. As they exited, the auditorium lights went dark, leaving the interior of the main building shimmering in the muted glow filtering through the stained glass windows.

Bryan set his bag in the corner, and pulling a heavy coat on, he said his farewells and was gone out the door. Jeff leaned the manger against the bag, and he adjusted the thermostat to its lowest setting.

"Ready for lunch?" He clapped his hands together with a smile. "Make sure you have everything. I'm locking up until next Sunday."

Katie was ready for lunch. When she stepped outside, she was pleased that the wind had died down. Except for the tracks left by the cars pulling in and out of the lot, and hard, compressed snow covering the street, everything was coated with white. Even the damage to the gazebo was hidden in the falling snow's sifted-flour wonderland.

"Apportez la voiture." Nicolette spoke the words quietly to Francois, who was in a plain suit rather than his uniform. He nodded and made his way outside.

Katie got that one. Francois was the chauffeur, and they were leaving. She expected her cousin had sent her driver to bring the car to the door.

It was only moments until tires could be heard crunching through the parking lot snow. Katie whispered to Winnie, "She told him to bring the car."

"Silly. I already knew that. It's what she says every time we go anywhere."

Katie huffed, but she wasn't angry. She was very pleased. Her best friend and her only blood relation had found a connection, and they were getting along like chums. Now if she could get Roker and Jess to wrap things up, life on the island would be cheery indeed.

And to think, three months before, she'd been stressed about leaving her Boston life behind. It didn't seem she was missing it much. Instead, it seemed Rockhaven life was exactly what Katie had been born for.

Katie was convinced as she had never been before. Rockhaven was her home, right where she wanted to be.

18

It was the sun breaking through the clouds that decided Katie she would play the part of Mrs. Claus with Jeff on the boat.

Being at Harbor View had helped.

Leaving the church, the sky had been thick, and the snow had blanketed the car all the way to lunch. Katie had ridden with her cousin and her friend, enjoying the unusual comfort of a pre-warmed vehicle, and the space that only a limousine could provide. As Francois moved out and onto the street, the big vehicle hushed the world outside, and Katie could have believed they were back in big-city Boston once more.

The landscape outside the windows told the difference. Spruce branches loaded with snow hugged the ground, and the houses along the way hunkered down, with great, thick roofs of cottony white. You didn't see that in Boston.

"Nikki? Are you feeling well?" Katie took her hand and squeezed it gently.

Once in the car, Cousin Nikki seemed to wilt. Although giving her a glamorous and poised appearance at the church, now her haute couture Sorbier served to highlight the contrast between the cutting-edge magnificence of the outfit and the elderly woman who wore it.

"Ah, ma chère." With her free hand, Nicolette patted the top of Katie's. "We feel so well as we choose to feel, is not it so? To answer, non. Cousin Nikki seems to have exhausted her day."

She smiled wanly and looked out the window, releasing Katie to place her hands in her lap.

Katie looked at Winnie to see her mouth, "She tires easily." Then Winnie pulled out her phone, and indicated Katie should do the same.

"Sweetie, it's been like this all week." The words appeared on Katie's screen when she tapped the text message icon. Then a sad-face icon appeared. "I haven't told you because I know how busy you are, and you haven't felt so well yourself." Winnie looked up and grinned impishly at Katie, patting her tummy twice.

"I've felt just fine today." Katie typed her reply text hard onto her screen, annoyed at the suggestion. However, even as she did, she was aware of why little Debsy had irritated her so much. She had felt just what Winnie suggested, and she hadn't yet used Nina's gift. She wasn't sure she wanted to know. Not for certain.

Not with Christmas coming in two days.

She tossed her phone back into her purse and turned to the window. The harbor appeared, and she realized the snow had stopped, and out across the ocean, lighter breaks in the clouds suggested the weatherman might be right for at least once this season. Wouldn't it be wonderful to have Jeff's Santa jaunt to come off perfectly this year? Especially if she intended to be aboard.

Nicolette didn't stay for lunch, with Francois explaining in fractured English that he must get Miss Nikki to rest, as the weather had absorbed her fuel. He only used three words, and Katie thought he meant the weather had sapped her energy, but the message was clear. She and Jeff would be taking Winnie either home with them or out to Nicolette's place. And it would be in the Jeep, because Katie's car was out there.

The Jeep had two doors, and Winnie could be the one to crawl over the seat and ride in the back. That was how Katie felt about that, and she had told Winnie so during lunch, only afterward realizing she had been irritated about her friend's insinuation in her text, and she had apologized for being curt.

Now Katie looked out into Moffat Cove to see her Katie tree firmly mounted to Jeff's boat, and he and Roker were attaching lights to the branches with plastic zipper ties. A box of small gifts was at their feet to hang on the tree. The cove was like glass, and all around, the snow on the shore made everything taller, thicker, puffier. Whiter, too, just like on a Christmas card. It was the perfect winter wonderland. It also made the red on the Katie ribbons stand out like a jolt of electricity, a series of glowing firebrands punching through the cotton candy to draw one's attention to the brightly wrapped presents that would soon adorn the tree.

Katie turned from the view and perused her clothing on the foot of the bed. She had every set of long underwear in her chest out, plus three pairs of socks, and an insulated jumper. She smiled at the array. Mrs. Claus would be a plump Mrs. Claus tonight. Her dress, a long, heavy, red affair borrowed from the Town Hall storage room, would have fit a person three times Katie's build. It was, she thought, literally, one size fits all. It came with a wide black belt to resolve that, and anyway, she would be hiding behind the tree most of the time.

It was Winnie's green elf outfit that was the humorous one. It came complete with oversized, green-striped shoes with long, curved tips, to slip over her own more cold-weather-appropriate footwear. Winnie had ranted, but Katie had been very matter-of-fact. Her friend didn't have a car, as she had left Katie's out at Nikki's, and Jeff had to be home by half past one. Oh, and we're stopping by the Town Hall to get my Mrs. Claus costume, and when I was in last week, I just happened to see a green elf suit hanging next to it.

The elf costume had an equal amount of room inside, as it was usually worn by Roker, who needed ample space for his ample waistline.

The sound of the living room door that opened to

the deck brought her back to the moment.

"Katie, we're about ready." The door closed with a firm thud, and the sound of feet on the wood floor said Jeff was inside.

"You don't know how much I appreciate this, Katie." That was Roker's voice, and it said he was also inside.

Jeff appeared in the doorway, and he glanced back into the other room with a grin before turning back to her. "I told him he owes us big time. I think we might get about two cords of firewood for this."

"You had better thank Winnie." Katie called it loudly, to make sure Roker heard. She walked to Jeff, running her hands inside his coat where he was especially warm, and hugging him. "He'd better, too. Otherwise, I might lose her for a friend."

"She'll have fun. By the time we get back, she'll be glad she went, and no way could we ask for better weather. No wind, plenty of sun, and lots of people looking forward to our visit." He chuckled and rubbed his hands over her back. "I love you, my Dame Katie. To find a woman who would enjoy this as much as I do, well, that took God, and I'm glad he brought you to me."

"Hey," she said, pushing away from him. "I get you out of the deal. I think we're pretty even."

"Oh, no," and he pulled her back. "We're not done here, yet."

"Oh?" She looked up at him, gazing into his eyes.

"Come on. Say it." He grinned.

Katie knew what he meant. His Dame Katie? He

was teasing her in the most endearing way, and he liked to be teased in return. She tapped him with her knuckle on the forehead just between his eyes, and she said, "I love you, too, Preacher Jeff. Now, though, Mrs. Claus has to get insulated, or she'll be in the hospital tomorrow with a bad case of frostbite."

She pushed away, and she stepped into the living room, calling loudly, knowing it would carry up the stairs, "Winnie? Are you dressed yet?"

"Katie!" The irritation was plain in the sound of Winnie's voice. "I can't believe you're making me do this!"

"Be a grown-up. And be sure to put on every bit of those underthings. You hear me?" She was still loud.

"The orange thing, too?" That was an old ski bib, again from town.

"Yes, the orange thing, too. It'll be under your green thing, and no one will see it." Katie saw Roker coming out of the kitchen with a piece of pie in his hands, and she looked hard at him. He was dropping crust on the floor. He disappeared back through the door.

"If I have to." That was Winnie, again, and then all was quiet from upstairs.

A timer dinged from the bedroom, either Jeff's or Katie's phone, telling them they had thirty minutes until launch. It was now two-thirty, and the sun would begin to sink below the mainland in an hour and a half. It would be very dark when they returned.

Thirty minutes was plenty of time, though, and as they gathered in the living room, they made quite a team. Winnie, beautiful as always in her green and white, and her striped shoes, rolled her eyes as she handed Roker her phone, showing him which icon snapped pictures for her photo album.

"If I'm doing this, I want it on Facebook. Winnie, the Christmas Elf. Who knows, I might get a Christmas gig out of it this summer." She smiled brightly.

"You mean next Christmas." Roker looked at Katie, making a face and nodding his head towards Winnie, as if she wasn't quite all there.

"She means summer. They shoot half-a-year out. I also want Jeff and me in a shot. Let me get mine." Katie's phone was in the bedroom, though, and before she could go after it, Winnie intervened.

"No, Sweetie. You come over here, and you, too, Jeff." He was just coming out of the bedroom, fully dressed except for his cap and beard. Winnie pointed to Roker, "You can take a bunch. Me, Katie, and Jeff, alone, and then all together. I want lots."

Katie sighed. She remembered a few she'd rather not have had put out there for the world to see. "Promise not to post mine?"

"Sweetie, I make no such promises. You hoodwinked me into this, so it's my right. Now, come here, and let's be beautiful together." She held out one arm, motioning Katie in.

"Yeah, let's be beautiful." Jeff was adjusting his beard, and he grinned at Katie. "Don't forget your hat, Mrs. Claus." He pulled a heavy, knit cap over his head, and he fitted his red and white Santa hat over it.

Roker snapped over a dozen, finally sorting out the

flash, and doing a few of those, also. Once she had her camera back, Winnie tapped away, finally declaring she had posted every one on her wall.

"That'll be a sight to see." Katie shook her head. "Now, to the float. We have presents to deliver."

"Can I take my camera?" Winnie held up her phone, giving a charming smile.

"You may not have any signal." That was from Jeff.

"That's all right. I can post tomorrow." Winnie seemed very pleased, as if posting what she did made everything right with the world.

Katie supposed it did. What had she said one time? When you store your memories in a photograph, that becomes your memory. Take a happy picture, and you always remember being happy at that time in your life. To judge by that, Winnie was having a very good day, even if she was dressed like an elf, and in a costume many sizes too large.

To tell the truth, she hoped her friend took lots of pictures, because she wanted to remember this, her first time out as Mrs. Claus, as the best time in her life.

Why? Because it was, absolutely, without question, the best Christmas that anyone could ever have.

19

They finally made it to the town float, where there were lanterns lighted, and about a dozen people waiting with their voices ready. They were dressed in bright, Christmassy colors, and against the powered-sugar icing covering the float and decorating the ramp, they were bright ornaments illustrating the joy of the holiday season.

Overhead the sky had dimmed into an orangey-red haze on the back side of the island, one that deepened into a deep cerulean blue overhead. A nearly full moon hovered on the horizon, as if given a special dispensation by the Good Lord above to light Jeff's and Katie's and Winnie's way along the shore tonight, rather like good will and peace on earth shining down from heaven above.

It helped that Jeff had full GPS navigation, and

every dock and underwater ledge was fully marked out. Even in complete blackness, there was no danger of running aground.

Kern had indeed been at the Peavey's, along with Brookie and Al and Janine's four. That had been one of Jeff's first stops. There were special presents to deliver, ones that crowded the boat more than was comfortable. They were from Al and Janine to their boys, direct from Santa, and the younger three had jumped up and down, their eyes shining with excitement.

"How's the plan working?" Katie had called to Kevie, giving him a big wave. He just grinned as he tore into his own gifts, ripping the paper away as fast as he could.

Pulling into the town harbor, Jeff remarked, "Finally, it's getting dark," as he throttled down the engine and eased the boat past the buoys marking the various ledges that might scrape the bottom of his boat. "I can see my way."

"See your way?" Winnie was getting into the elf thing, and she had her phone out snapping shots of everything she passed. "I can barely see in my camera anymore." As she said that, the flash went off, and she looked at the screen. "Oh, that one turned out okay."

It was a shot of one of the Katie bows that decorated the tree now set up and anchored on Jeff's boat. With the flash, the string of Christmas lights formed little more than bright fireflies against the tree.

"Oh, oh, I have signal. I can post!" She began frantically tapping at her phone, nudging Katie and whispering, "Why does Jeff want it to be dark? It seems he could see the rocks better in the light." To keep from sinking was also clear in her question.

"I can hear you, Winnie. I don't mind telling you." Jeff looked at her and grinned, as they approached the town float. "It's not seeing the rocks, it's finding the docks I need to stop at. I look for lights and head that way, and I can skip the rest. I don't exactly get notifications of who's going to be on which dock."

"He does have an idea, though." Katie made a point to whisper in a loud stage voice, just to tease Jeff. "There are seventeen stops on the list, plus anyone else who just happens to make it down to a dock."

One they hadn't visited yet was the De Groot dock. It was a massive granite monstrosity out near Katie's place on Carver Point, and some of the original family had come out to spend the holidays. That was the airplane she and Jeff had heard. Katie had wondered if the family still owned it, and she was very pleased to find it still controlled by the family she'd met when she was still a "summer" girl all those years ago. It gave her back a sense of permanence, as if people who settled on Rockhaven stayed on the island, and homes lived in and loved in continued to be filled with that love forever and ever.

Katie needed that, with the empty foundations at her place on the Point.

Yes, they had an idea of which docks they would visit, and those on the docks had a rough idea of when Jeff might be by. The Santa voyage took hours, and it wouldn't do for people to be forced to stand and wait in the growing darkness and the bitter cold that would settle across the island once they were in full dark. If that was the case, there would be no participants at all. They would all be huddled inside, warm and cozy, leaving Santa to fly overhead, and purchasing their gifts online for Dyer's Delivery to bring to their door.

Kent and Nina were two of those on the town float, brightly festooned in their seasonal best, and festive when contrasted against the softening backdrop of the fresh snowfall. Jess was there, too, and Roker, who'd driven in to spend the evening with the woman he'd finally begun to notice. Babbitt George was there with his wife, together with Mara, their teenage daughter, in tow. The adults got boxes of chocolate candy, or canning jars filled with cocoa mix, if they preferred, but Winnie pulled gifts from the tree for the children.

Katie didn't know all the people, as her church family were the ones she recognized. However, no matter who had gathered, they did have to sing for their gifts, a Christmas song of one sort or another, either religious or secular. This group sang as a choir, a rousing rendition of *Jingle Bells*, albeit with many mistakes, and several breaking into laughter and pushing at the shoulders of yet others.

The song was what Katie expected. Even from the entrance to the harbor, they could be heard practicing, their voices starting and stopping, as whoever was leading them tried to correct misremembered verses and melody lines, ones that never did quite fall into place.

All in all, the evening went wonderfully. The De Groots down at the dock were unfamiliar to Katie, but she welcomed them, anyway, and the house was fully lighted. In that, Katie knew someone had brought electricity out. Running the lines was expensive, and that meant they could afford to keep the place up. Ada Parkes-Simpers? Once again, someone had to be last in line. She was out waiting, though, and she sang a very emotional *Away in a Manger*, a solo for the Santa team, and Mrs. Claus cried by the end. It was beautiful, a single caroler, wrapped in her winter warmth, standing on her pristine, snow-fluffed dock, and singing a capella under the light of a Christmas moon.

Even Winnie said she'd never seen anything so beautiful, and she'd taken a picture to post to Facebook as soon as she got signal back again.

She did complain about taking Ada's cocoa mix up the ramp, but that was to be expected. Winnie loved the glamor and glitz. It was the legwork that poked a hole in her holiday enjoyment. However, Katie reassured her as she stepped from the boat onto the float, there were never seals out at this time of the year. They only ate little green elves in the middle of the summer.

Winnie had laughed lightly, as if she discounted Katie's reassurances, but Katie was fairly certain she heard her friend humming *Rock-a-bye Baby* as she stepped back onto the boat.

It was as could be expected: And fun was had by all.

20

Monday, Christmas Eve, dawned late, because it was the end of December, and cold, again because it was the end of December. It was also beautiful outside, once more because it was the end of December.

Who would not want to live on a Maine island on Christmas Eve?

Francois arrived in the limousine to retrieve Winnie. “Mademoiselle Nicolette, um, need your presence, s'il vous plait.” He was in his driver’s livery once more, all formal and officious, even in his roughly phrased English.

This morning Katie didn’t care one whit whether Winnie stayed or went. She just wanted to survive. It was the night of the Town Hall Banquet, catered, if she understood it correctly, by Kent and Nina. The Town Park displays belonged to everyone. The Christmas musical rested firmly in the arms of the church members. This? She had claimed this as her own. and she wanted it, her first real Christmas bash on the island, to come off perfectly.

If she didn't throw up, first.

"Go, go." She was curled on the sofa, wrapped in a throw, and trying to make it to lunch. "Sorry!" She leaped to her feet and ran for the bathroom, slamming the door after her.

"Sweetie? Are you sure?" Winnie knocked on the door. "I can't leave with you sick."

"Jeff's here. He'll be inside in a bit. He can look after me." He and Roker were undoing what they'd done the day before to Jeff's boat. The Katie tree was returning to the dock, and the boat was being readied to haul lobster pots once again when Christmas wound down. Having an income was important, and Rockhaven Town Church? It was a small town, and that told how well that paid.

Katie didn't want to open the door and face Winnie. Instead, she looked at herself in the mirror. How could she feel so bad? She opened a drawer and pulled out the box Nina had slipped into her coat pocket the day of the sailboat races. It stared her in the face. Pink or blue, she didn't know, but if she saw the line, dear God, that would explain a lot. She looked ceilingward. Please, God, know what you're doing.

Another knock startled her.

"Sweetie? What should I do?"

"I'm fine. It's just indigestion. Don't forget about the banquet tonight, and give Nikki my love." She tried for a bright sound to her voice.

"I won't, and I will. Bye-bye, and I'll see you tonight. It's a busy day." Winnie finished brightly, thrumming her fingernails on the door; and it went silent. It was hardly any time at all before there was another knock on the door.

"Katie?" It was Jeff.

"I'll be out in a minute. I'm just finishing." She made sure her voice was bright this time.

"Winnie said you didn't feel well. Are you certain we don't need to call the doctor? Maybe we should cancel tonight."

"Ha, ha." She said it as two separate words, not as a real laugh. "That's Winnie, always thinking everyone's sick. She's not getting out of the banquet that easily. She promised, and I'll be there to make sure she comes through."

"If you're sure."

"I am. How'd the boat go?"

"It's all taken care of. If you're really all right, I might run with Roker out to Neil Foote's place. Roker got word his generator went out during the night, and that's his only power source for his heater. Are you okay with that?"

"Go. I'm fine." Or she would be, in about six months, if this was what she thought it was. Besides, she knew Neil. He barely got around anymore, an old island landmark who'd been old when Katie was a girl. If she remembered correctly, his generator ran only the blower on his oil heater, one similar to theirs. He probably had a wood stove, and propane, but his heater would be oil. Without electricity, it was dead in the water.

"The Jeep's here if you need it, and the keys are on the table. Bye. I love you, Katie."

"I love you, too. Enjoy your day."

Katie was relieved to have the house to herself for a while. She felt somewhat better after her recent bout of nausea, but it would be easier to deal with this box alone. She thought Jeff would be pleased, but they hadn't discussed it, not seriously. It was more looks when Al and Janine's kids were going crazy, and the looks said, not now, not ever!

The test was as simple as the box said, and once it was over, Katie sat on her bed and looked out across the water. Their lives were going to change. Big time. Al and Janine big time, and she wasn't sure that was a good thing. Would life be a Debsy life, little more than unplanned trips to the potty, or a Matt, huddled under a tree to chuck rotten snowballs at passersby? Oh, dear God, she thought. Why are you doing this to me?

Distraction, she thought. She needed distraction, not to sit here and think about this all day. She stood, relieved to be feeling passably well, and she headed for the kitchen and the car keys. She would make her way to the Town Hall and see how the banquet was coming along.

Her car would have been a better choice. Katie knew that as soon as she began to move down the drive. Jeff's off-road beast sat high, and the big tires, while great for traction in the snow, did nothing for stability in the cockpit. She was glad to reach the paved road to where the surface was relatively level.

The road was an empty ribbon of white, with little more than tire tracks and curbs of sugar-iced greenery to indicate the asphalt underneath. She pulled out and headed toward town. In Boston, this would be one of the busiest shopping days of the year. Here? There were no malls or big boxes on the island, so if it wasn't already bought now, it wasn't going to be. Island people were at home, enjoying their holiday, except for Winnie, she hoped. Her friend had promised to be at the Town Hall preparing the banquet for the evening. A special Christmas surprise, she'd said to Katie the day she and Cousin Nikki arrived.

If Winnie came through, this would be the best surprise her friend could give her, to take this day off her shoulders and make it a grand success. Katie wanted to see what Winnie and Nina had dreamed up.

Pulling up to the Town Hall was the first suggestion that something wasn't quite right. There was no one there, not one car, and not one light on that she could tell. The snow was as fresh and new as yesterday's snowfall, with only one set of tracks from their quick stop the day before to pick up last night's costumes, telling her no one had entered or exited the building at all today.

She parked and got out, stepping gingerly through the thick snow. She tried the door, with no success, and stepped to the window to find the blinds drawn. Pulling her phone from her pocket, she tapped Winnie's number and listened to it ring. It immediately sent her to voicemail, and in that, Katie knew her friend was out of range. She left a message anyway, telling her to call, because she was at the Town Hall, and there had better be a banquet tonight. She would have slammed the phone down, except she couldn't. All she could do was press her finger against the end call icon.

She wiped at one eye. The box, and now this. Sniffling, she touched Jeff's number, only to have the same thing happen again. She said she loved him, and she hoped Neil's heater was working fine.

Driving through town, Harbor View was closed, but Katie expected that. Who was out on Christmas Eve, except the frustrated minister's wife? Tire tracks told her someone had been there, but even Kent and Nina's car was gone.

Katie pulled to the side of the road and rubbed her forehead with one hand. Her nausea was rolling again, and she didn't feel like driving out to Nikki's to look for Winnie there. The night before was so perfect. It was the way Christmas was supposed to be. How could Winnie let her down in this? Katie had invited everyone who wanted to come, and now?

Now, all Katie wanted to do was cry.

ORPHAN HOLD
DO NOT SHIP

H1 – 000000000278

ISBN 9781943189052

CLIENT	Alternate Sourcing
STATION	TPP Receiving Station 03
HELD	2026 – 10 – 08 08:55

SHELF

If its order arrives, scan this label at a receiving station.

21

"Katie Carver here." Katie laughed, holding the phone away from her face for a second. "My apologies. Katie Ragsdale, here."

She had laughed, but she didn't feel happy at heart. Nervous? Silly? Maybe even stupid? All those fit. Happy? Not by a long shot.

And Jeff hadn't come home. Even the sun outside her windows hadn't cheered her. It was a relief when she heard his voice.

"I always knew you were still my Dame Carver."

"Jeff, where have you been? I left you a message, and I haven't heard back." After the first surge of relief, she felt irritation rise. Why hadn't he called back before this?

"I apologize. After finishing at Neil's, Roker and I had another errand to run. Have you been out today?"

"Once." Now she was even more irritated. It was Christmas Eve, he should be here with her, and he was out running errands for everyone else on the island. He hadn't married them. He'd married her. It was self-pity. She knew that. She also knew she deserved her self-pity. She had been abandoned, and Boston was looking pretty good to her right then.

Anyway, he didn't sound very sorry, and out? Why had he asked her that? He'd left her the keys.

"Where'd you go, Katie?"

"What's this?" Her irritation was developing claws. "Is there someplace I'm not supposed to go?" Like, to town, maybe to the Town Hall, maybe to see that Winnie really is a flake, and she's going to make a promise, then decide she likes fashionista Nikki better than me, her best friend?

"I thought you might like Janine to come by to keep you company while I finish my errands."

"Janine!" Katie melted at the mention of her name. Her boys, and all Katie could see was having four just like them, and all at one time. Quadruplets! In the wintertime! Throwing snowballs with rocks, and how high would their doctor bills be then?

"Not Janine?" For the first time, Jeff sounded concerned. "Um, I need Jess, but, how about Jackie? I think Tom can take over for Jackie for the rest of the afternoon. Do you want Jackie to come over?"

"Oh, I don't know. It's just that it's Christmas Eve, and I miss you—" The front door rattled with the sound of a repeated pounding fist. "Someone's at the door."

"Ahh, too late. That's probably Janine. Honey, you two have a good time. I'll see you tonight. Bye, bye. Love you." And he was gone.

Katie groaned, standing, and she looked through the glass doors. Sure enough, there stood the diminutive mother of four, and she waved and smiled when Katie stepped into view.

"Katie! Look what I brought!" Janine bustled in when Katie opened the door, and she had a foil-covered pan in her hand. "This is my grandmother's favorite recipe, and I want your opinion on it."

"We'll sit in the kitchen." Katie couldn't work up any enthusiasm for food. She wanted Jeff.

"Look at you." Janine stopped and looked carefully at Katie's face. "You look beautiful. Al told me that once, when I got pregnant with Kevie. Before he even knew, he told me one night I was beautiful. The other three, pah! They were just muffins in a pan. Come on. I need your help."

Katie had to take a deep breath. Oh, Janine. If only you knew. She put it aside, though. She had to. When she said something, Jeff would be the first to know. Not Janine, although telling this friend seemed the best choice if she did have to spill the beans, so to speak. She would understand.

By then Janine was rooting through Katie's cabinets, and Katie was trying to keep up.

"A stool. I can't reach your top cupboards. Jeff has this serving platter, footed, like a rectangular cake stand. It was his mother's. Do you know it?'

"Pink glass?"

"I would have said rose, but pink will do. Sort of iridescent. You know where it's at?"

"Here." Katie reached over the fridge, and she pulled it down. "We've not used it since I've been here." She hadn't even known it was special in any way, just old. And it had one chip out of the foot. It needed to be kept turned to the back to hide it.

"Sit that down." Janine motioned, and she set the covered dish right in the middle of the table. "This is to die for. Does that phrase date me? Ha. Now, this, though, is the best thing you've tasted in your life. Baklava."

With a flourish, she whipped off the foil, and there, in one of the Harbor View's pans, was a gleaming pastry cut in a diamond pattern. Katie knew it was Harbor View's, because it was embossed on the handle. Harbor View. Rockhaven Maine. Not for Sale.

"This is your grandmother's dish?" Katie tapped the words on the handle. "And my stomach's been, well, I don't think I could eat any right now."

"Oh, the pan?" Janine laughed, as if making light of the pan and Harbor View's name. "My oven's out. Sorry. And it's not really baklava, but that's the closest thing I know. It's good, though. I need you to help me arrange it."

By the time they were finished, Katie wondered how many ways there were to arrange little diamond pastries on a pink iridescent footed serving platter with a chipped foot. Apparently more than she'd ever dreamed possible.

"I have to take this to a get-together." Janine dug

in the drawers and found some plastic wrap. She whipped out a long piece, and she tucked it in and over the diamond sort-of-baklava artfully displayed on Jeff's mother's platter. "Come on. You can ride along. No kids." She chuckled.

What else did Katie have to do? She shrugged and pulled on her coat, not the least enthused, and she didn't try to hide it.

"Now, don't be a grump. This is for an elderly lady, and she can't come to pick it up." Janine smiled cheerfully and pulled Katie out the front door. "In my car, and we won't be gone long."

Long was subjective, Katie decided, sitting in the seat of Al's truck, and holding the serving dish with the almost-baklava in her lap, as they drove through town, and headed towards the north side of the island. Town Hall? Still deserted, and that depressed her. Heading past Harbor View, she saw her blue Volkswagen, and she frowned at that, irritated. What was Winnie doing there? She reached for her phone, only to realize her purse was at the house. Janine had said not long, so she didn't say anything. Even so, she planned to bite when she got close enough to Winnie to leave good teeth imprints.

Finally, Janine turned on her blinker, and Katie had to say something.

"This is my Cousin Nikki's place. I mean, she's only rented it for two weeks, but why are we here?"

"Oh, I need to drop off something." Janine smiled, waved her hand dismissively, and tugged at the steering wheel of the big truck to swing it into the drive.

"It's bumpy, so hold on to that dessert."

It was towards the end of the drive that Katie grew suspicious. Cars lined the roadway, Corrine's and Roker's. Jess'. There was Tom and Jackie's in the trees and out of the way. Jerry Watson's and Kayline Stryker's was blocked in by Bobbitt George's. And more. They were everywhere.

Inside was where it became real. When Katie stepped through the door, holding her almost-baklava, a good portion of the town and the entire church membership stood in front of the massive glass wall that made up the back of the home, and they yelled with all the gusto they could muster, "Merry Christmas, Katie! We love you!"

"Merry Christmas, Sweetie!" Winnie yelled from the far side of the room, where she stood by Cousin Nikki, next to the most massive Christmas tree Katie thought she'd ever seen inside a private home.

Jeff handed the baklava off to someone else as the people dispersed into smaller groups and began talking, and he wrapped Katie in his arms. "My Christmas gift to you. Everyone's pulled this together for you, as a surprise. And it's catered by Harbor View, so we know it's going to be good."

"I thought—" Katie was choked, and she didn't know what to say. "Then, Neil—"

"Really needed his heater repaired. Did Janine keep you busy?"

Katie shook her head. He had no idea. "I drove to the Town Hall, and I thought Winnie had forgotten. Then you didn't come home, and it was Christmas

Eve." She felt her eyes tear up, and she refused to cry. People might think her unappreciative, and it was Christmas Eve. She had to be bright and festive!

"I had no idea! Katie, Katie. Winnie cares about you. She would never let you down, and neither would I. Promise."

Katie laughed, more to disguise her embarrassment than anything else. A voice across the room distracted her.

"Joyeux Noël!" The voice was cracked, but it was strong, and across the room, Cousin Nikki stood with Winnie's and Francois's help.

"Everybody!" That was Winnie. "Everybody listen up!"

When the talking quieted, Nikki continued. "My only surviving relation, ma chère Katie, has brought me to your wonderful America, and I welcome everyone to my home. Please, please have a merveilleux and Joyeux Noël."

"Forgive me?" Jeff had her wrapped in his arms once more.

"Of course, and always." Katie took a deep breath, and she knew she meant it. What could be better than this, a Christmas Eve spent with family and friends, and held in the arms of the man she loved?

It was indeed the most wonderful present anyone could have planned. It showed Jeff's love to her in every possible way it could, especially when he kissed her, long and hard, right there in front of Cousin Nikki's massive Christmas tree.

22

Katie opened her eyes. The room was darkened, with small slivers of early morning light coming in around the blinds. She knew what day it was, and she buzzed with anticipation. Christmas Day on Rockhaven. Her first one ever.

Jeff lay at her side, his shoulder touching hers, the warmth of his body bleeding through his pajamas. His face, the morning stubble she adored, and his eyes, closed in sleep. Christmas sleep. The best sort, the kind that happened only one morning a year. The kind that could only happen one morning a year.

She slipped sideways from underneath the bedding, and she made her way to the living room, gently closing the door behind her. On one side were the gifts brought by Nikki and Winnie, all the way from Boston, still waiting to be unwrapped. Katie was sure they had brought enough for everyone on the island to have at least one. The other direction, the blinds on the windows were all raised, and just at the horizon, the sky was a rosy-pink band of color, lifting the ceiling of the earth as the day peeked at the world to see if it was time to wake.

"It's Christmas!" the sky seemed to say. "Wake, World, and celebrate the birth of the King!"

Katie shivered with the unfulfilled expectations of the day. Christmas! Life couldn't get any better.

She pulled out her phone, and she tapped a number. It picked up, and a sleepy voice spoke to her.

"Hello?"

"It's Christmas!"

"So it is. The sun's barely up. Let me sleep till nine."

"Honey, it is almost nine. Well, eight. It's Christmas!"

"The sun comes up at four."

"In the summer. It's Christmas!"

"Call me when it's time for lunch. Merry Christmas." The phone went dead.

Katie smiled, but she wasn't letting Winnie's lack of enthusiasm put a crimp in her Christmas plans. Last night had been for the entire island, but today was for her family and closest friends. Plus, she had a special gift to share with Jeff today, and she wanted everyone here when she did.

It was the kitchen that took up the next few hours. Her most prized concoction? Her pumpkin pies, fresh from the real thing, following Jess' instructions. Add to that a chocolate cream, something new and untried, just for Janine's boys. The turkey came prepped for the oven, directly from Nina's kitchen. Everything else would arrive with her guests, enough to feed everyone, and probably plenty left over. Like the Bible story of the loaves and the fishes, bring a little, take home a lot.

Putting on the coffee finally pulled Jeff from the bed, and he wandered in, giving Katie a sleepy kiss, and wandering back in the living room to wake up a while. He called out a belated, "Merry Christmas," as he began to rumble around, making a fire.

Winnie had demanded a two o'clock lunch, saying she would never make it before then, but Katie's guests began arriving by ten. Roker, first, and Jess at the same time. Their addition to the feast? Another pumpkin pie. When Katie showed her two already prepared, Jess said she remembered the story of the pie on the day of the storm, and she wanted to ensure that Roker had plenty. Then she pulled out some of Nina's eggnog, already chilled and ready to drink.

Janine had the four boys with her, coming in about noon, and telling her Al would come later. Even on Christmas, there were errands to run, and loose ends to tie up. Something for Jeff, she whispered, pulling Katie aside. I'm not supposed to say anything, so don't mention it.

Katie shook her head, thinking it must be good if Janine couldn't keep it inside. She'd done pretty well the day before. Katie hadn't even guessed, not until they were halfway up the drive.

She didn't expect Cousin Nikki until Winnie arrived. Katie let Jess and Janine take over her kitchen, and she joined Roker, Jeff, and the boys in the living room. The men were stoking the fire, although to Katie, it looked as though they were playing to see how high they could get the flames to leap. Occasionally the wood sparked, and one of them would stamp the ember or kick it back on the hearth to let it die out.

Even the windows got into the festive spirit, steamed up with the joy of a houseful of Christmas guests, that and pies, turkey, and all the other things being prepared in the kitchen.

The boys were preoccupied with their hand-held gaming systems. Katie watched them for a time before realizing they were playing each other. When she asked Kevie about it, he told her, without removing his eyes from the screen, "Bluetooth, and we can't talk," and he continued his game.

"Bluetooth," Katie said to herself. She understood Bluetooth. It was a way of connecting without connecting, although that wasn't really right. It was a way of connecting when there was no connection system available, when there was no Wi-Fi set up. It was a local connection, and it only worked when the devices were close together. If one of the boys carried his game too far away, the connection was lost, and he was no longer part of the action.

Like Babes and Ritchey and Austie. Apple. The Reynolds twins, Bennie and Bobby. The island pack she and Jeff had run with as children. They had been Bluetoothed, then they'd spread too far from one another, and the connection had been lost. She'd wanted to return some of that connection for Jeff, to reunite him with his best friend from childhood, but that was the one thing that hadn't come together for her. Why, even Kevie, no longer believing in Christmas, had leaped in with both feet and made it real for his younger brothers. Everything else had fallen in place, except for the Bluetooth.

Still, it was a pretty good Christmas all around, and perfection? Sometimes good enough was the best life offered.

Roker was bringing in more wood when he pointed out the first sign of something unusual.

"Jeff, you know of anyone flying in today?"

"Not that I'm aware."

"Come see." Roker stepped outside, closing the door when Jeff joined him.

Katie walked to the window, and wiping a spot clear, sure enough, there was a small plane, and it seemed to be looking for something. The one she and Jeff had seen before hadn't come to this end of the island. It was too far out of the way. At one point, the craft flew close enough to the house to read the lettering on the wings. It dipped one of its wings and flew off the direction of the airport.

"Was it important?" Katie quizzed them when they came back in, stomping their feet.

"It was odd, I'll say that." Jeff peered through the glass where the craft could be seen in the distance. "Why would it fly over here? Hey, Roker, who do you think's unlocked the airport?"

He shrugged, as if it wasn't important. However, to

Katie, it did seem important if someone was landing there. She understood the question. The "airport" was little more than a level field, and it had a locked gate so the local teens didn't tear up the field by doing donuts in the middle of the night. Anyone landing there would need someone to get a car in and out.

It was nearly two by then, and the boys were getting restless. Katie was about ready to eat, too, and those pumpkin pies? Katie was certain her guests needed something to tide them over before they attacked those.

"Hey, everyone, it's Christmas day. Jess brought over some of Nina's specialty eggnog. Thank you, Jess." Katie pulled her from the kitchen and gave her a one-armed hug. A round of applause echoed in the room. "To begin, let's start off with that. Jess, do you mind pouring?"

They were still on the eggnog, serving the final cups, when someone banged on the front door. The windows that direction were equally misted with all the people and the cooking going on, but the door wasn't locked. Anyone knocking knew they were to join the festivities.

"Ah, we can eat!" Katie called to her guests, expecting their new additions to invite themselves in. After all, Winnie and Al? They were as much family as friends. "The rest of the Christmas feast has arrived. I'm not sure what they brought, but I'm certain we'll enjoy it very much."

Janine came out of the kitchen at Katie's speech, and she fought a smile. Roker was doing the same.

Even the four Peavey boys had ready-to-burst secrets written all over their faces. Katie saw, and she looked to Jeff to see if he knew what was going on.

Jeff shrugged, and he turned to Roker. However, before he could question him, the door banged again.

"You gonna get that?" It was Roker. "You, Jeff, with Katie, why don't you head to the door?"

Katie hesitated, looking to Janine's boys, but each one in turn shook his head and sank back in his seat, smiling all the while. She looked to Jeff and held out a hand. "Preacher Jeff? Shall we answer the door?"

"Sure, Dame Katie. Everyone else is too lazy." He chuckled, and he led his wife through the first glass door and through to the second. Opening the door was when they understood, from Winnie's suggestion of a Christmas surprise, to Janine's whispered secret, to the mystery plane in the sky. Even Al's absence fell into place when Jeff opened that door.

A man Jeff hadn't seen in nearly ten years stood there, and he held out his hand. He grinned with just a bit of an embarrassed smile, and he said, "Hey, Jeff. I've missed you wicked bad."

"Ritchey? Hey, man, what are you doing here?" Jeff looked like he couldn't get his head around the man's sudden manifestation on his front step.

When Jeff reached to grab the hand, the man laughed, and he grabbed Jeff in a bear hug. He slapped him hard on the back, this time saying, "Oh, man, I've missed being here more than you can know."

"Ritchey?" Katie looked to him, then to Winnie and Al helping Nicolette out of her atrociously long limousine. As she watched, its lights flashed, and it began to turn, moving away from the house.

"And you, I would know you anywhere, Katie Carver. Winnie showed me pictures of you, but I had no idea you'd become so beautiful. Maybe I should have stayed around." Ritchey laughed and gave her an equally big bear hug.

That wasn't all, though, for about then, another man stepped around Al and slapped his hand on Ritchey's shoulder, and he wore a cap festooned with embroidered pilot's wings. He pulled Ritchey out of the way, and grinned a broad and winning smile.

"Don't forget about me. This turkey wouldn't be here if I hadn't come along. Did you notice that wing dip? Just letting you know we saw you."

"Austie! Man, you were willing to fly this guy? In the same plane with you? You are a sucker for an ugly face." Jeff grabbed Austie William's hand, and he threw an arm across his neck. "Welcome back."

It was Ritchey he couldn't keep his eyes off of. Katie noticed that. And Ritchey was focused on his old friend, just like old times, like two handfuls of years had melted away, and all it had taken was one simple hug.

"Do we get to come in?" That was Austie's question. He still had his arm across Jeff's shoulders, and he gave him a mock punch to the stomach. "I remember being king of the world with you. I should at least get to come into your house. Besides, you've got more company coming." He pulled Jeff in and said that right in his ear before leaning around and pointing to Katie.

"And you. I thought you were beautiful at fourteen. Hubba, but look at you now."

"Yeah, yeah. Come on in." Jeff elbowed Austie as he shook his head and looked away from Ritchey's face. Except for one brief glance when Austie walked up, Jeff broke eye contact with Ritchey for the first time. He had a smile on his face that wouldn't go away.

The four of them crowded the foyer, making room for Winnie, Nicolette, and Al. As they passed, Winnie said, "See, I can keep a secret. Merry Christmas, Sweetie." Nikki said a simple "Joyeux Noël." Al? He handed Jeff a set of keys, and he said, "Thanks, pal. I locked the airport back up. You get to keep these."

When everyone was past, Jeff grabbed Katie in a full hug, and he whispered to her, "Thank you, Katie. This means more to me than anything. I love you so much. I knew you weren't telling me something, and now I know what it was." He kissed her several times on different parts of her face.

"Jeff," Katie cautioned, beginning to laugh. "Jeff, I had nothing to do with this. I'm as surprised as you are."

"Then?" He stepped back and looked in the living room. "Not Winnie?"

Katie shrugged. However, she thought so. She just didn't know how.

23

"Attention." Nicolette tapped the side of her glass with a knife, and the sharp sound quieted the room. Francois had been playing the role of butler, and he was unobtrusively clearing dinnerware away. Nicolette waited until he was out of the room, and she motioned for Jeff to help her stand. "Is magnifique to spend this day with family." She lifted her glass, and she motioned to those around the room. "And friends who come as family. We spoke in the car, and of my friend, Winnie, I know more, but I would that everyone hear. Please. Stories!" She raised her glass to clapping and cheers, before gingerly returning to her chair.

"Yeah, Ritchey. You first. Your wife? You? I'm at a loss how you can be here." Jeff shook his head, and while he may have been at a loss, the look on his face didn't include disappointment. "Bare your soul to everyone here."

The two men had been telling old stories, with embarrassing ones about Austie, including the story of the rotting clams that they'd had to dump in the harbor when they couldn't sell them. Austie had turned red with embarrassment. However, that had been the simple renewal of old friendships. Now with Nicolette's demand, it was time for the real stories to be laid bare.

"My wife, my wife." Ritchey ducked his head and ran his hand through his hair before he looked up. "You've met Tricia, but not Allie and Mark. They're five and three now. Of course, we have the new one, why I couldn't make the wedding."

"So you'd said." Jeff seemed to find relief in Ritchey's casual reference, as if it had bothered him, even having known, and now he could let it all evaporate undiscussed.

"You know from before why Trish isn't here. Boats!"

"I remember." Jeff laughed, glancing at the ceiling for a moment. "But you are. Not to stay, I'm sure, though I'd be happy if you didn't leave too soon."

"Trish is at her mother's until the first, so I have a week. The wife rules the life." He shrugged, even as he kept his eyes on his friend's face.

"You just what, decided, and on Christmas? Spill, dude, spill."

"You know Katie and I have been keeping in touch." He nodded Katie's direction.

"Katie?" Jeff looked to her. "How, and when?"

She shrugged, and she smiled. It was the sermons, but Jeff hadn't wanted her to bring up Ritchey, so she hadn't. Now was not the time to go into that.

"The real reason I'm here? It's that girl." Ritchey pointed to Winnie. "Stuff happened, now she's up to be the face of my stores. You'll soon see her in all my adverts. Since she has a connection here—" He pointed to Katie and Jeff. "—I got to thinking, and I decided to buy that old place on Main, you know, just down from the Harbor View. Expansion is the name of the game. I'll be right next to the Post Office. Perfect location, and it wouldn't have occurred to me without these women. Hey, Kent and Nina still run Harbor View, right?" He looked around to judge people's responses.

"You just ate their turkey." Katie said that with a smile. She was remembering why Jeff had bonded so tightly with Ritchey. He was charming everyone in the room.

"Ah. That's why it was so good, not to impugn your cooking, my good Katie." He smiled at her. "That's my story. Austie? He's my man. You want to tell it?" He held his hand out as an invitation.

"I'm good listening to your version." Austie gave it back to him with a laugh.

"My man there flies the skies for what, American?" When Austie shook his head, Ritchey shrugged and went on. "Anyway, I offered him a free weekend up here just for flying me, and here we are. Two old buddies, catching up on old times on the way up. Now, three, four, five old buddies." He pointed to each of the old pack that was in Jeff's house.

"I can't stay, though." Austie rapped the table a couple times in an unconscious motion. "Tomorrow I have to be in Bangor to catch a flight to St. Petersburg. Off to the Sunshine State. I'm not really a snow person."

"So you're stuck with me." Ritchey pointed to Jeff. "And I want my old room. Remember how we used to stay in that little room with the bunk beds and sneak out at night?"

"I still have those bunk beds." Jeff's grin was back. "They're yours anytime I can convince you to visit."

Katie couldn't contain herself any longer. She stood and wrapped one of Jeff's arms in hers, and she waited until everyone looked at her.

"Katie?" Jeff lifted her hand and kissed it. "Yes?"

"I have a present I would like to announce." There were call-outs and clapping, and Katie felt her face warm. "Jeff thought I was keeping a secret from him, and that it was Ritchey. Ritchey, you I didn't know about, but that bunk bed is yours anytime you want to come visit. I'll stand behind Jeff's invitation. Never think it's not open, with or without advance warning. However, I have been keeping a secret. I'm pretty sure Nina guessed, but I asked her to keep it quiet, and it seems like she did. Jeff, this is for everybody, but it's really a present for you. In about six months, as close as I can judge, you're going to be a daddy."

"That's why you've been sick?" He looked like he was in shock. She nodded, and he threw his arms around her and hooted. "Oh, that's the best news I could ever hear."

The room broke into several minutes of animated conversation and high-handed slaps of congratulations. Winnie threw her arms around Katie, saying, "Oh, you girl, you can always top everything I do. This one's the best one of all. I get to be Auntie Winnie. You have to promise!"

Cousin Nikki began tapping her glass once again. When the room quieted, she got Jeff to help her stand once more, and her voice shook with emotion as she began to speak. "For years my sister and I were separated by an ocean. She was stolen from me, and I wish to give my family back what was lost. Katie, ma chère, will you accept a gift from me?" She held out her hands, and Katie reached and took them, to have Nikki draw her into an embrace, a real one. When they separated, her cousin had tears running down her cheeks.

Katie looked into Nikki's face as she said, "You coming to Rockhaven for the holidays has been gift enough. You being here has given me back much of what I lost. I couldn't ask anything more." She meant it, too.

"I wish to give you back your home. Will you accept such a gift from an old woman?"

"I'm confused, Nikki. I have a home. Right here." Katie glanced at Jeff to see him shrug.

"Non, I wish to give you back your grandmamma's home. Then, your new little one can make the memories you know so well."

"I don't understand." Katie knew what she thought Nikki was saying, but the funds to rebuild the old place? The cost would be staggering.

"Just say thank you." Jeff wrapped her in his arms. "It's Christmas, Katie. It's the season for giving, and today, everyone gets exactly what they want. Everyone. Everything."

Katie looked across the room, and she knew Jeff was right. Here, on this isolated island in the middle of the ocean, in this one room, she had everything she had ever wanted. God had given her Jeff and their baby, and Winnie, and all her friends here. Roker, Jess. Al, Janine and the boys. Then God decided it wasn't enough, and He opened His hands, and in stepped Nikki and Ritchey and Austie. Now, she was being given her childhood home back again.

All this, and they still had a mound of gifts to unwrap. It would be fun, but the best one had already been offered and received.

Katie took Nikki's hands, and she leaned in to give her a kiss, telling her that having her grandmother's house back again was the best gift anyone could have given her, ever.

"Non," Nikki replied. "Your gift to your Jeff is a gift to me, also. You give me back life. It is the best gift of all."

"Your Cousin Nikki is right." Jeff pulled Katie in, and he gazed into her eyes. "Your gift is the best Christmas gift of all.

Then he topped it off with a Christmas kiss, one that was cheered on with gusto by everyone, both large and small, young and old, in the room.

As they finished, the boys cried out, not quite in

unison, but certainly in chorus, "It's time for Christmas gifts! Can we open ours now?"

It was, just as Katie had hoped, the best Rockhaven Christmas ever.

www.ingramcontent.com/pod-product-compliance
Lightning Source LLC
Chambersburg PA
CBHW061543250926
52052CB00010B/3045
9781943189052